The critics praise Diane Salvatore . . .

"*Love, Zena Beth* follows *Benediction* with a bang . . . Salvatore's writing carries us along from the goose bumps of hero worship to the hot flashes of hedonism . . ."   *Booklist*

"Salvatore's bold account of a lesbian relationship eloquently conveys the anticipation, passion and doubt within any love affair, straight or gay . . . Soulful, candid and refreshing, this erotic novel challenges the perception of homosexuals (and women) as 'others,' and explores love's impact on friendships and careers."   *Publishers Weekly*

"Salvatore has a great eye for detail . . . *Love, Zena Beth* is a highly entertaining novel . . . Ultimately [it] is a book about . . . self-knowledge, power, sex, relationships and fame, written with humor and honesty."   *The Los Angeles Times*

". . . should secure its author ever-widening circles of acclaim . . . the lovemaking scenes are a joyous celebration of female sexuality . . . Salvatore strides along at a pace which is all swagger, swank and gay abandon."
                    Australian Bookseller & Publisher

". . . wonderful . . . a steamy, sensuous sensation . . . an amazing, captivating book on so many different levels . . . the sex is phenomenal . . . a rich narrative . . . rewarding reading–from its examinations of human relationships to its no-holds-barred eroticism."   *Deneuve*

". . . whirlwind . . . terrific thigh-squeezing sex scenes . . . a novel about obsession, fame . . . and betrayal . . ." *Lambda Book Report*

". . . a great book . . ."   *Dimensions*

DIANE SALVATORE

NOT

TELLING

MOTHER

STORIES FROM A LIFE

NAIAD
1993

Printed in the United States of America on acid-free paper
First Edition

Edited by Katherine V. Forrest
Cover design by Catherine Hopkins
Typeset by Sandi Stancil

Library of Congress Cataloging-in-Publication Data

Salvatore, Diane.
    Not telling mother : stories from a life / by Diane Salvatore.
        p.   cm.
    ISBN 1-56280-044-2
    1. Lesbians—United States—Fiction.   I. Title.
PS3569.A46234N67   1993
813'.54—dc20
                                            93-24911
                                                CIP

for my parents,
with love and gratitude

About the Author

Diane Salvatore is the author of *Love, Zena Beth* and *Benediction,* which was nominated for a Lambda Book Award as Best Lesbian Fiction in 1991. She is also a senior editor for a national magazine.

DEVOTION

Renee smoothed Number 8 sunscreen over Celia's freckled back with crisp efficiency. She knew from experience which areas would be most vulnerable to the sun's high beam, where it would leave a telltale scorch of red, like an iron forgotten carelessly on silk, if she didn't distribute the cream uniformly and with patience.

Edie and Cole, and the new couple, Jan and Maggie, had dashed directly down to the water after spreading their towels and digging holes for their thermoses. Edie was Renee's comrade, dating back to their college days. Spared the complication of having been lovers, breaking up and making up again, they had always been nothing more — or less — than friends. Later, when they both took their first serious lovers, it was just incredible good luck that Renee liked Cole, and that Celia liked Edie, that Cole liked both Renee and Celia, and so on.

The house they'd rented for this July week slept six — eight if you counted the pullout in the living room as a reasonable accommodation, which the real estate agent did and Renee did not — and Edie had suggested, at nearly the last minute, that they invite another couple, Jan and Maggie. To defray the costs, she explained, and, Renee thought in a moment of peevishness, to put a kink in the predictability of their Provincetown vacation, which had featured just the four of them for the past five years.

It was one-half of each couple — Cole and Jan — who returned first, collapsing onto the blankets like shipwrecked sailors who'd been uncertain of rescue. "It's freezing," Cole announced, squeaking her palm over her wet blonde hair. "A school of fish floated by in a block of ice."

Jan smiled slowly. "She's exaggerating," she informed Renee and Celia, who had settled into low beach chairs alongside the blankets. Renee had decided her prone-on-the-potholed sand days were over and was grateful for the civilized comfort of the canvas chair. "It's not bad," Jan said, "once you get under."

"I can't believe Edie's still out there," Renee said, squinting into the horizon which was trafficked by huge black dragonflies. "She's usually the one with the least tolerance."

"She's trying to out-butch Maggie," Cole said, rolling onto her back and grimacing into the sun.

"Maggie doesn't seem the type who'd be hard to out-butch," Renee said carefully, not sure if this observation about her lover would offend Jan.

"Oh, but that's the type you have to watch out for," Jan said, looking toward the waves for her lover. "Femme on the outside, butch on the inside."

Renee felt a prickle of irritation work over her brow. She didn't know Jan well enough yet to be able to gauge how seriously she took such labels. This was how they were bound to get to know each other, though, tossing out categories to define themselves: Democrat or Republican, native New Yorker or import, lawyer or social worker. For now these handles would take the place of intimacy, which could only be established spontaneously, in tiny bursts of surprise: what would draw a laugh in watching an old rerun, how hard a debate over guacamole ingredients would be fought, or the way a drunken late night phone call would be received. But all this would come later, as Renee and Celia got to know Jan and Maggie better, *if* they got to know Jan and Maggie better, given how delicate and volatile couple-chemistry could be. They might remain Edie and Cole's friends alone, the way Eileen and Chrissie, by some unspoken agreement, remained Renee and Celia's alone.

"This I have to see," Renee said, hauling herself out of the chair. The heat tended to make her inert, her limbs as heavy as lead, so it helped to have excuses to keep moving. She ran down to the waves, squashing sand under her heels all the way. She let the water lap at her feet, experiencing it not as

3

liquid but as pure pain, entering at the ankle and stabbing its way up her legs.

She spotted Edie and Maggie to her left, diving head first, their bodies arched like dolphins, into wave after wave. Edie had on black shorts and a black bikini top; Maggie was one sleek swath of white spandex, her legs long and toned as a runner's, but her hips and breasts full and rounded, not the rectangular proportions of most athletes. Renee watched her slice into the waves as if they were benign as buttercream. Edie, struggling to her feet after being battered by one, grasped Maggie's shoulder for balance.

"An athlete in her own mind," Renee called over to them. They turned, at the same moment, and started waving vigorously. "Don't get me wet," Renee warned sternly as they began to advance.

"It's gorgeous, like bath water," Edie said, winking at Maggie and pressing an arm across Renee's shoulder blades.

"*Don't!*" Renee shrieked, reduced to schoolyard pleading. "I'll *kill* you!" Maggie nabbed her kicking feet and soon she was swinging, deaf to her own screams, through the steel-blue sky and into the icy wall of the next wave.

Everyone was back on the blankets by the time Renee had summoned enough good humor to rejoin them.

"That's it, you're out of the will, both of you," she said, falling into her chair next to Celia. "And it's a damn shame, because the rubies would have gone so well with your coloring."

Edie gave her an exaggerated look of forlorn remorse. "Are you okay, really?" she asked in baby-voice.

"Lucky for you I took my heart pill this morning," Renee said, clutching a garish, scratchy beach towel around her in the manner of a nursing-home resident.

"Honey, you're scaring Maggie and Jan," Celia said. "They think you're serious."

"Last time we bring the kids to the beach," Renee muttered, unwilling to relinquish her martyred role yet.

"I'll get revenge for you, Renee," Cole said, grabbing the back of Edie's neck and shaking her, just as she was taking a swallow from the thermos. Edie choked and coughed elaborately.

"Well, time to shed the house-arrest look," Jan said, lying rigidly on the towel. "Wake me when I look Navajo."

"Darling, none of us will live that long," Maggie said, leaning down to kiss Jan's white-blonde hairline.

Renee retreated behind her sunglasses, happily anticipating the monotony of the coming week. They would spend their days joking and gossiping and burning on the beach, their nights eating lobsters and prowling Commercial Street for bargain T-shirts and earrings. She was even beginning to feel cheerful about Jan and Maggie being along; it would make their routines seem novel all over again.

Celia offered a can of soda, beaded and slippery with condensation, and as Renee turned to take it, she saw Maggie unhooking the top of her white one-piece, letting it fall forward as unself-consciously as she might turn the page of a magazine. Her breasts, already light brown, sprang free full and firm, and as she rubbed lotion in circles over them, her nipples, clay-colored and large as half dollars, puckered into points. Renee felt a stake of desire drive painfully through her ribcage straight down to her groin, followed closely by the aftertaste of melancholy. She no longer welcomed such stabs of interest in other women; the stirrings no longer attracted her curiosity. They were as inevitable, pointless and uncomfortable as indigestion, and she'd just as soon never have an attack again. She turned to Celia guiltily and tousled her dark blonde curls. "In vacation mode yet?" she asked.

"Day one of brain-dead existence and loving it," Celia answered, balancing her own soda can on the armrest of her chair and staring out at the water like the captain of a ship that was miraculously on course.

After dinner, Edie asked Renee to join her for a walk. Tonight they had barbecued at the house and Renee, not much of a cook, compensated by doing a lot of the cleanup. After a day under the hot breath of the sun, the slightest bit of manual labor wore her out. She would have much preferred to sink into the couch and read, or join the game of poker that Jan and Maggie, and Cole and Celia had started on the deck. But something about Edie's tone made the walk seem required, not optional.

The night air was fragrant with the scent of salt water and honeysuckle, and cooler than she thought it would be. She quickly regretted not having thrown on her windbreaker. It probably didn't help that she'd gotten slightly burned. Her skin felt hot to the touch, as if lit with a flame from the inside.

Renee did most of the talking for the first few blocks, as they strolled past the other guest houses at the far end of Commercial Street. Edie gave uncharacteristically clipped responses.

"So, do you like Jan and Maggie?" Edie asked suddenly.

"Sure, aside from Maggie helping you nearly, send me to an early grave. But I admit I was a little jealous at the beginning and now I think it's actually fun to have a bigger group for a change."

"What do you think of Maggie?"

"Maggie?" Renee remembering the bathing-suit top fall away, felt her face color and was grateful for the cover of nightfall. "I like her, I guess. It's too soon to say. I'm still absorbing them as a couple."

Edie stuffed her hands into the pockets of her baggy plaid shorts. Her short dark hair had dried oddly after her hurried shower; the top looked as though it were straining into a mohawk.

"We're having an affair," Edie said softly, prayerfully.

Renee stopped walking; fear coiled in her stomach. Edie was a few steps ahead before she stopped, too, and turned.

"Well, don't look so appalled. It happens. It happens to people all the time."

"What do you *mean?*" Renee said. "What are you

talking about?" Edie might as well have told her that the sky was orange or the beach had turned into snakes.

"What do you *mean*, what do I mean? Are you going to make me repeat it?"

"What I *mean* is, are you crazy? Are you in love? Are you leaving Cole? Does Cole even know?"

Edie shook her head and started walking again, burrowing her hands deeper into her pockets. Renee could see the shape of her fists bulging against her thighs.

"Don't walk off all wounded," Renee said, catching up and grabbing her by the shoulder. "What did you expect me to say? What exactly did you drag me all the way out here expecting me to say?" Edie just kept staring at the sidewalk, offering only her frowning profile. "I mean, my God, I've known you and Cole together now longer than I've known you alone."

"And is that what friends are for? Judging you? Making you feel bad?"

"And what did you think they were for? Giving a stamp of approval to every idiot thing you do?"

"Would you lower your voice, *please*? If I'd wanted Cole to hear our conversation, I would have just stayed at the house." Edie was hitting the pavement with her heels as though she meant to break it.

"You know you're going to have to tell her," Renee said. "It's just a question of sooner or later."

"Later, then. I don't know what I'd tell her if I tried to tell her now."

"What does Maggie say?"

"She and Jan have been rocky for almost a year. She'd like me to leave Cole."

"Jesus Christ! Does it matter what *you'd* like?"

"You just asked me what Maggie'd like!" Edie was facing her now, her dark eyebrows lowered in a scowl, her lips pursed like a school teacher regarding a particularly dense student.

Renee walked ahead. She was aware of the swell of panic in her chest. Sometime past age thirty, she had crossed a line where change had become her enemy. Change could only mean decline, some circumstance worse than the ideal that had existed before. Edie had always been the restless one, the one who charmed Renee into the next adventure, the next scheme. Renee suspected it kept Edie charged if she could get her to go along, because she helped Edie work for every thrill. What would it mean now if she couldn't cross this line with Edie? And what would it mean if she could?

Edie caught up and walked silently alongside her.

"You know, it's not as though you're unique, that we don't all feel it," Renee said. "You're with someone a while, things get predictable, a little boring. Some other woman catches your eye, laughs at your jokes. But you don't just jump on every one, you know, you just don't —"

"I haven't, for God's sake! I've never cheated on Cole before."

"So why now? Why Maggie?" Renee seized Edie's elbow. She had to know the answer. Knowing would be an antidote for all her own unruly desires.

9

Knowing would make the threat definable, would give its outlines limits, would make it seem conquerable.

"I have no idea," Edie said. "Maybe just circumstance, opportunity, one beer too many. I was at work one night, late — this was a month ago. She called me, said Jan was away and she was a little stir crazy, and could I stop by on the way home. I called Cole, said a bunch of us from the office were going out and not to wait up for me. I don't know why I lied before I even had to. I guess I knew it looked odd, Maggie making the invitation the way she did. It wasn't that I went there knowing something would happen, or even that I *wanted* something to happen, but I just didn't want to explain it." She turned to face Renee. "I just wanted this something — whatever it was going to be — all to myself. I wanted to get back to a place where I was just *me*, where I wasn't just one side of a Siamese twin, when every time you lean over, the other side comes with you. You know what I mean?"

Renee looked away. She did know, but she decided that Edie didn't deserve the acknowledgment. There was such a long distance between having those feelings and acting on them. Or at least she had always thought so. "And then what happened? When you went over? I didn't even think you two were especially close."

"We weren't. That was probably part of the formula. Maybe she felt she could risk it. If we drifted apart because I was shocked and turned her down, it wouldn't have been such a great loss. Because she wasn't looking for a friendship from me.

She wanted escape, and she needed it in the form of a lover."

"She just propositioned you, just like that?" Renee was convinced that the mystery was in the details, that if she had all the tiny moments of it, the larger meaning would reveal itself.

"Of course not," Edie said, shoving Renee lightly. "She started telling me how she and Jan weren't getting along. She didn't know what to do. She was afraid to leave and afraid to stay. She started to cry and the next thing I knew, we were on the couch together and —" Edie stopped and sat down on the cement steps of a shop that was closed for the night. She leaned her back against the darkened glass door.

"And?"

"And we had the most incredible sex." There was no boast in her voice, only sadness. "I haven't felt that way with Cole in years. Years." Edie hung her head and it was that gesture of misery that kept Renee from walking off in disgust, that kept her rooted to the spot, hopeful that there was some way back to the way things used to be.

"And you think that's the most important thing?" Renee put one foot up on the steps and leaned in.

"No. I mean, what I really mean is, I know it's not *supposed* to be." She looked up, a child admitting to breaking her mother's favorite vase.

"And after five years with Maggie, the sex wouldn't be so incredible anymore, either," Renee chided. "That's just brain chemistry — pheromones and dopamine and stuff you can't control. You're not supposed to base a life decision on it. Don't you get it?"

"But nothing replaces it. Nothing else feels the same way."

"Well, if that's the way you feel, then maybe you'd better leave Cole now. Then you can be sorry later."

Edie's head snapped up. "Who elected you the monogamy moderator, anyway? I can get this lecture from my local priest."

Renee was stung but didn't let it show. They had arrived at some sort of impasse. Edie seemed completely foreign to her at that moment. She felt that she could walk away now and not wonder about her ever again for even a moment. Unless she spoke now, pushed past this patch of strangeness, she feared she might do just that.

"And I'd thank you to do the same for me if I ever lost my mind and did this to Celia."

"With pleasure," Edie said sarcastically.

Renee sat next to her on the steps, a new horror occurring to her. "The absolute worst thing, the part I can't forgive you for, is inviting them up here with us. And only telling me now. It's one thing for you to lie. But now you're asking me to lie to Cole, too."

"Oh, it's not like that," Edie said, unsnapping and snapping the metal latch on her watch band. "She wouldn't consider it your place to tell her. She'll hold it entirely against me, don't worry."

"Whatever possessed you, though? How am I supposed to act around them all week? How am I not supposed to look at Jan as though I've just been to a psychic and know that she's about to be in a car wreck?"

Edie ran her hand over the top of her dark hair. "You'll manage, like I am."

Renee stood. "It's the most selfish thing you've ever done. It's worse than the affair itself. How can you stand it, having them both here? Making fools of Cole and Jan? Not to mention me and Celia."

Edie pressed two fingertips to her closed eyes. Renee could tell that she wanted them both to pretend she wasn't crying. "I wanted to tell you before," Edie said. "I was afraid."

"Because you knew how I'd take it."

Edie nodded. "But then I thought it might help. If I told you. I thought you would help me."

"I can't. I can't help you with this." Renee got up and started down the block briskly enough to let Edie know not to follow. Now she would have to think of some explanation why she was returning to the house alone. It would be just the first lie.

Renee woke up feeling water-logged with sleep. Celia, her hair flat from sleep, was propped up on pillows beside her, reading. The low-ceilinged room was lit with the pale glow of early sun, but the air still had some of the chill of last night's dampness.

"How long have you been awake?" Renee asked.

"About an hour." Celia leaned down and kissed her. "It's nine o'clock, sleepyhead. The beach awaits. It's a beautiful day."

Renee rolled onto her side, pulling the sheet up to her chin. She and Celia had radically different attitudes about sleep. Celia considered it something to be tolerated, to be gotten through and over with as soon as possible. Renee found it one of the most sensual indulgences of life, but that was probably

13

because, during the week, commuting from Brooklyn to Manhattan for her 10-hour work day, she got only about six hours of it a night. We are doomed to lust after what we can't have, she thought glumly.

Celia put her book aside, stretched out and raked her fingertips along Renee's stomach. They had made love last night, the first of the vacation, and the first time in nearly two months. Renee always found, once they had started again, that the craving, easily buried under a million daily distractions, was still there. She missed Celia, missed gliding her palm down her sloping back to the swell of her hips, missed the slippery, unhurried kisses. She still felt the clamor to please her, still felt the hot press of urgency at discovering Celia wet for her. But even when they didn't make love at home, Renee was attuned daily to Celia's body. She liked to smell her scalp, to knead her back, to kiss the warm and delicate skin of her eyelids. Who had decided that none of that mattered, none of that counted, none of that was sex?

"Maybe I don't want to go to the beach," Renee said, all five-year-old petulance.

"Would you rather go on a whale watch?"

"I don't know."

"What's the matter? You've been moody since last night. Did you and Edie have a fight?"

Renee had thought of nothing else since their walk except whether she should tell Celia Edie's news. Now she realized all she had been doing was trying to decide when to tell. She usually failed spectacularly at keeping secrets from Celia.

"She's having an affair. With Maggie."

Celia's fingers stopped moving. "So Jan was right."

Renee turned around, trying to read Celia's light brown eyes for meaning. "Jan *knows?*"

"Not that it's Edie. But she told me she was pretty sure Maggie was having an affair. She's confronted her, but Maggie's denied it."

"Good God — when did she tell you all this?"

"Yesterday, at the beach. When the two of us walked to the bathroom."

"She told you on the way to the *bathroom?*"

"Well, it was close to a mile walk, round trip," Celia said. "And obviously she was looking to get it off her chest."

"What did you tell her?"

"Tell her? Not much. I mainly listened. No one can tell another person what her bottom line is. I have no idea if she's the kind of person who wants to wait out an affair, or if she's the kind who considers that grounds for homicide."

"You know which kind I am, right?" Renee pulled Celia closer, squeezing their breasts flat between them.

"You never fantasize?"

"About what?"

"Don't be coy." Celia pushed a few inches of space between them. "About being with another woman."

"You know about all my crushes. Sometimes before *I* know about them. That's all they are." She ran her hand through Celia's soft curls. "Why? Do you?"

"You knew about Phyllis." Phyllis was a woman at Celia's office with whom Celia used to have long, raucous phone conversations at night from home.

15

When Phyllis left to go to another company, Celia admitted she was relieved. She had begun to worry that she was getting too caught up, and the woman wasn't even gay. "That's all that's ever lasted more than ten minutes."

A burst of laughter exploded from the direction of the kitchen, followed by the clink of coffee mugs against the counter.

Renee rolled onto her back, punched the pillow into a mound under her head, and stared up at the ceiling. "I feel rotten. I can't face Cole."

"Why don't I go out and tell them you feel sick? Shoo them off to the beach without us. Then we'll do something alone. And whatever else we decide, it'll be your turn to tell them."

Renee wished she could lie in bed forever; it was the only act that really was no decision at all. Staying away today was mainly a stall, but she knew Edie would take it as a betrayal. She tensed as Celia smiled, reached for her silk robe, and padded out toward the kitchen.

"Hey, you feeling better?" Edie shouted as she slammed the car door shut. The four of them, returning from a day at the beach, had their arms full of towels and thermoses, beach bags and chairs. They trudged wearily toward the porch, where Renee was swinging slowly in the hammock.

She rested her book against her stomach and watched their advance. Jan had bright red stripes down the front of her legs and arms, as if she'd been

16

spray painted on the run. Maggie and Edie still had shiny wet hair; they had probably dashed in for a last splash right before they got in the car. Cole was doing a moonwalk; no doubt she'd fallen asleep on the beach and wasn't fully roused yet.

"All recovered, buddy? Celia give you some tender loving care?" Edie said, loud and jovial, stopping at the top of the porch stairs and giving the hammock a little shove with her beach-slippered foot. She was getting her trademark summer tan, a tan that made her look more fit and handsome.

"A clever ruse," Cole said, struggling to release her wet ponytail from its tie, "to get the house all to themselves for the day."

"You're on to me, Cole. As always," Renee said, watching Edie's blue eyes narrow in a silent warning.

"You guys go on ahead," Edie said. "I'm going to sit out here and make sure Renee's recovered enough to be having so much fun."

They all shuffled obediently into the house. Renee couldn't be sure if she imagined it, but she thought Maggie gave her an appraising, anxious look before she let the door close behind her.

Edie pulled one of the recliners over. "It's going to be pretty hard to avoid us all week." She was nearly whispering, watching Renee's face like a patient scrutinizing a doctor about to deliver critical test results.

"You can relieve me of trying if you just do the right thing."

"Which right thing is that?" Edie brushed her palm back and forth over the back of her hair, apparently trying to dry it.

"Tell Cole what's going on."

Edie looked away, scowling. "Or end it with Maggie, is what you really mean."

"I know you can't do that yet. And I wouldn't believe you if you told me you had."

"I don't tell you how to run your relationship." Her voice was flat and gravelly.

"And I don't ask you to be an accomplice."

"God." Edie shook her head. "I don't understand. You and me, we've always told each other everything. Why are you blackmailing me now?"

Renee looked away from Edie's pained face. "Because it's different now. There are other people I care about involved. There are consequences. You asked me to put my loyalty to you above everything. Even my own principles. That's not devotion. That's something else, something warped — I don't know what."

Edie rubbed her eyes; when she dropped her hands back into her lap, Renee saw that she was crying. "So what are you going to do? Are you going to tell Cole behind my back?"

"I thought about it, about telling you that I would tell her if you didn't. But then I thought maybe that was too easy — for you, I mean. Maybe you even unconsciously wanted me to do that for you. Because you couldn't."

Edie waited.

"So Celia and I took a room over at one of the little guest houses down on Bradford. She's waiting for me there now. We spent the morning packing up and looking for places with vacancies. But you have to sort this thing out on your own. I don't want to be a witness, and I don't want to be a guilty bystander."

"You moved *out*? You're kidding, right?" Edie had drawn her knees up to her chest, was hugging them so hard her knees were nearly white.

"It was the best plan I could think of. To salvage as many relationships as possible."

"It doesn't salvage ours at all," Edie said. "That's a goddamn declaration of war."

"I knew you'd think so now. But I have to hope that maybe you won't always think so."

"Unbelievable," Edie said, clutching at her sides as though she were about to be sick. "You didn't even give me a chance to think about what you said, to think about telling Cole or anything."

"You've had a month to think about telling her. It wasn't my place to put a gun to your head."

"Which place are you at? What's the name?"

"Let's just leave it alone for this week, Edie."

"Jesus, just like that. Just like that you can turn your back on me?" She began to pick at the frayed edge of one of the recliner slats.

"That's not what I'm doing. I'm saying I can't play this charade with you. And I won't."

"And what am I supposed to tell everyone, about why the two of you are suddenly gone?"

"You'll manage, like I am." Renee smiled as she used Edie's own phrase against her. "Anyway, that's the least of your problems. But they'll probably believe that you and I had some kind of fight. You can tell Cole it's something I asked you not to talk about. That should buy you some time."

Edie leaned forward, straddling the recliner,

rocking slowly back and forth, her arms folded against her stomach. "God, how did things get so screwed up?"

"It's a mystery, isn't it? Things just happen to you." Renee eased out of the hammock.

"It's like you're making me choose between you and Maggie."

"That's not the choice, Edie, and you know it. Don't be perverse."

"That's what you think, isn't it? That it would be perverse to be with me. You're jealous, aren't you? You can't understand why Maggie would even want me."

"I'm going to do you a favor, Edie," Renee said, walking down the weathered porch steps. "I'm going to leave before we get to finish this conversation. Because I want us to pick up where we left off after you get your life in order." She waited an agonized moment for Edie to say something and when she didn't, she turned and started away.

"Who can you count on," Edie shouted at her back, "if you can't even count on your friends?"

Renee forced herself not to turn around. She kept both hands in the air, over her head, not sure herself if the gesture meant surrender or goodbye.

THE VIEWING

The nun was old, they told us, and we did not have to go see her if we didn't want to.

My best friend at the time, Penny Fitzgerald, said she wanted to go and dared me to come with her.

I'd had a crush on Penny since we were six years old and sat together under a crab apple tree and she'd unbuttoned her white ribbed school blouse and let the wind blow it open. Her chest hadn't looked much different from any of the boys who ran around shirtless all summer, but I was electrified all the same, though I'd had no idea why.

If Penny was going to see the old nun and dared me to ("You're not creeped out by some shriveled old dead nun, are you, Renee?"), then I was going.

My mother was skeptical when I asked for permission, which the school said we had to have in writing; she did not think I was ready for such an encounter. Because of that, she had spared me from my great-uncle John's wake the year before, but I assured her I was much more mature by now and besides, I was going to have to start getting used to these things. "Is that so?" my mother had said, looking up from the checkbook she was writing in, and I nodded, all nine-year-old gravity and seriousness. I could not explain to her — or to myself — that somehow the idea of seeing the dead nun had gotten twisted up with Penny Fitzgerald's breasts and the warm, itchy feeling they had given me. I had no choice but to go.

All the girls who were going were excused from math period that day, since math and "the viewing," as the nuns were calling it, were both at 10:00 a.m. Missing math, of course, was so desirable that to accomplish it, plenty of girls would have gone as far as watching a live frog get dissected, and this is what accounted for the fact that nearly the entire class of twenty-eight fifth graders was going. Sister Patrice lined us up, a virtual conga line of neon-colored parkas with navy and gray plaid uniform skirts sticking out the bottom, and led us out of the school and down the block to a brick building between the church and the rectory.

"It smells funny in here, like moth balls," Penny, in line directly in front of me, hissed over her shoulder. She made a gagging face.

The smell was only incense, and too many years of not opening the windows wide. I did not object to the musty, overheated airlessness of the place; it actually had a kind of comforting effect on me, the way the smell of my mother's chicken gravy did. Sometimes this alarmed me and made me wonder if that meant I was destined to be a nun. But I did not dwell on this now. I shuffled forward with the rest of the girls, single-file, till Sister Patrice, stout and pinch-lipped, told us to come to a stop in front of a dark green velvet curtain. It was pulled back, and we could see the flicker of a huge candle, the kind that was put on the altar for Easter and Christmas Eve. We could also see one end of the casket, shiny black like a limousine.

"Now girls, this is a most solemn occasion, but not a sad one," said Sister Patrice, folding her pudgy hands together in front of her. "All good Christians look forward to the day of their death, because it means they will be reunited with their Maker." She squinted out over the line of us from behind her thick, round glasses. "Sister Mary Helena taught girls such as yourself for forty-five years before retiring, and though we shall all miss her, we rejoice with her now while she enjoys her reward of everlasting peace in the Kingdom of Our Lord. As you approach, observe a moment of silent prayer and form a line to the left."

Penny turned to glance at me, and I thought she looked a little green beneath her auburn bangs, but I couldn't be sure, since the light in the place was so

23

strange. Ahead of us, Sharon Walsh abruptly did a side step out of line and stood, her shoulders bobbing, till Sister Patrice came around and led her away to the left. It seemed both courageous and cowardly of Sharon to back out at the last possible moment, and even though I was sure that every girl in line felt sorry for her and wished they could join her, later we would have no choice but to mercilessly tease her, punishment for the unspoken offense of not helping us beat back the grip of terror.

The rest of us shuffled toward the candlelight and casket, and held our breath as girl after girl disappeared behind the curtain. Occasionally, one girl would break into a sloppy, hiccoughing sob, and Sister Patrice would have to make another end run to retrieve the traumatized student from behind the curtain. She began to look annoyed, I thought, that we were making a mockery of her speech about this being a happy ceremony, not a sad one; her movements grew more and more sharp-angled and brisk.

"Renee, I don't know if I can do it," Penny turned to whisper.

I had no words of advice for her. I was feeling colossal dread myself, but the march forward had come to feel inevitable, inescapable. I felt a prisoner of it as completely as I would have if strapped into a roller coaster as the car crept its way up the first incline. So I clapped my hands together in prayer and shut my eyes, which Penny must have taken as encouragement, because when I opened them again, she was no longer in front of me and the green curtain was rustling.

My heart had swollen to three times its normal

size, I was sure, and it was beating against my chest like a lightning bug in a jar. My cheeks felt steamy, my palms sticky; I desperately wanted my mother. For a fervent few seconds, I considered joining my fate with Sharon Walsh. But the temptation was abruptly cut short: suddenly there was a loud thud from behind the curtain. Someone in back of me screamed and that started off several others; soon the line had dissolved into chaos and girls were running everywhere. "Omi*god!*" someone shrieked. "She's rolled out of the casket!"

I rushed behind the curtain, nearly colliding with Sister Patrice, and found Penny crumpled on the shiny wood floor, her legs bent at unlikely angles, her arms sprawled in an unruly pattern. Sister Patrice blessed herself as she nodded to Sister Mary Helena, then shoved her arms under Penny like a lifting fork, and carried her off. "A fainter," I heard her mutter, and that was the only thing that kept me calm as I turned to look at the frozen face of the dead nun, chalk-white and sunken-cheeked, looking more like a mannequin than anything that had once been human. She had on a royal blue habit, a little swell of shellacked white hair sticking out from under it. She looked starched and antiseptic, and I found it impossible to imagine what she had been like in life, to imagine how emotions might have animated her face. She looked to me very dead, like someone who had always been that way.

In stark contrast to Sharon Walsh, who was persecuted as predicted, Penny became something of a celebrity for the rest of the year. For one thing, no one had ever seen a real person faint. Maybe we had seen it on *I Love Lucy* but surely not in our own ordinary lives, and surely not among our very peers. Everyone wanted to know what it felt like, if you could feel it coming on, and if it was something that could be learned and done on cue (the uses for which seemed boundless to many). As the weeks went by, and Penny seemed to sense that interest was flagging, she began to embellish, to confess that, though she had been too shaken to admit this at first, what had really triggered the fainting spell was that she saw Sister Mary Helena open her eyes. She hadn't been sure at first, she reported; after all, she knew how overwrought we had all been. ("Overwrought" was the word the school nurse had used to explain things to Penny's rattled mother.) At first, Sister Mary Helena's eyes had opened just slightly, but then they flew wide open and she stared — scowled even — right at Penny. The next thing Penny knew, she said, she was in some back room with Sister Patrice shoving a foul-smelling something under her nose.

I didn't believe the story for a second — and I wasn't sure the other girls did, either — but I admired the way Penny held sway over us nonetheless. I considered briefly somehow inflating my own role in the rescue, but I found that I did not have the same gift of hyperbole and self-promotion that Penny did. I recognized even then that this was a social handicap, and would leave me in the position of envying outsider too many times in life.

I asked Penny about it the next Saturday I was at her house. We more often met at her house rather than mine because her mother let her and her four brothers have two guinea pigs. The brothers had to be tolerated in order to share access to the pungent, slovenly animals who seemed more intent on shrinking from us than anything else. Penny's mother had only that morning caught two of the boys, Peter and Timmy, trying to get the guinea pigs to eat peanut butter and lap up vodka – and had forbade them from any proximity with the pets for the next three weeks.

"I won't tell anyone," I said to Penny. "So you can tell me the truth. I know you didn't see Sister Mary Helena open her eyes." I tried for supreme nonchalance in an effort to encourage candidness.

Penny fell back onto her bed and made her arms and legs stiff and lock-jointed. "I did, too. She even turned her head toward me," she said, demonstrating.

I rolled my eyes to make it clear I was not taken in by this, but also that I did not care enough about it to try to discredit her publicly.

Penny lifted herself up on one elbow. "Didn't she scare you, too?" she asked.

I took this as a semi-confession and, feeling emboldened by her trust, risked taking the topic in a whole new direction. "I felt sad," I said.

"Why? Because she was dead and all?"

"No, because I felt like no one probably ever really loved her."

Penny gaped at me. It was clear she thought it freakish to contemplate nuns and love – apart from the religious kind – in the same sentence, let alone in the same realm of possibility. But romance was my latest, and secret, preoccupation. I had taken to going to the public library and hunting down the

27

steamiest-looking covers on the Young Adult shelves. It hadn't yet occurred to me to venture into the adult section; I had great and unquestioning respect for the way the library was organized and would no more have violated its internal logic and rules than I would have gone naked in public. The latest book I had read involved a girl in love with a boy who smelled of Ivory Soap and took her on sailing trips with his parents, and the whole bunch of them wore outfits with creases pressed into the sleeves and slacks. Everyone smiled a lot at each other and shared various pleasant compliments. It seemed to me that all the nuns ought to have a chance at such a wholesome experience, much the same way they might go for a swim or visit the zoo, at least once before they devoted their whole lives to God.

"Timmy told me all the nuns are lezzies," Penny said, sitting bolt upright on her plaid bedspread, "and all the priests are homos. That's why they don't mind living together the way they do and not getting married."

Timmy was three years older than us; I did not take information imparted by a twelve-year-old lightly. Goose bumps rippled all up and down my neck and arms.

"Do you know what a lezzie is?" Penny said, just a shade taunting, eager, as we all were then, to catch the others with any remnant of babyish behavior. But we were city kids, fairly sophisticated. Most of us had heard or overheard definitions of any number of scandalous types — alcoholics and molesters and whores and homosexuals — fairly early on, from one source or another, or heard at least enough to form a negative impression.

"Of course I know," I quickly said, not sure at all, and certainly not making even the slightest association between the word and any of the things I had felt about having been stirred by Penny's six-year-old breasts all those years ago under the crab apple tree.

"Well, so, maybe her and Sister Patrice were lezzies together," Penny said, folding her arms across her chest with the finality of a pronouncement.

"No way," I said, getting up from the floor to look out the window. I was a little embarrassed to be defending the old nuns, one of whom I hadn't known at all and the other about whom I felt no particular fondness. But it just seemed the right thing to do, to defend them against this accusation.

"All I know is, as soon as I'm eighteen, I'm going to marry Mark McDonough," Penny said. She got up and fussed with her bangs in her bureau mirror.

I hadn't quite learned this game yet, but would over the next few years, this game of selecting one of the boys as my secret heartthrob, and planning my fantasy wedding, right down to the number of bridesmaids and the number of children to follow. I was never good at it, which is to say I never learned the right pitch of hushed enthusiasm and awe, but none of my friends noticed, so caught up were they in shouting out their own imaginings. They even earned my amazed respect after a while, so varied, particular and extravagant were the dresses and processions, so byzantine the politics of the maid of honor choices. Of course, minus the giggling, the girls would sound very much the same way ten or twelve or fifteen years later, planning their actual weddings, when the world, by then, would have taken on a whole new configuration for me.

"How can you know you're going to marry Mark when you haven't even had a date with him yet?" I asked. "When you haven't even had a date with *anyone* yet?"

"You'll see. I just know, the same way I know that Sister Mary Helena and Sister Patrice are lezzies together."

This became the new wood Penny threw on the bonfire of her local celebrity to keep the rest of the girls in thrall. In this round, Penny claimed that before the smelling salts (as she had learned by then they were called) had completely brought her around, before she had actually opened her eyes again, she had heard Sister Patrice crying and saying, "Oh, Mary Helena, what in Lord's name will I ever do without you?" The girls were horrified and riveted, and a few of them grew completely spastic in Sister Patrice's presence. I never challenged Penny about this again, especially not in front of the other girls, because it had occurred to me by then that even if Penny had thought she was making this part up, too, she might actually be remembering it.

Penny Fitzgerald did grow up to be Penny McDonough. She and Mark, who drove a bread route, had three boys and got divorced when the youngest was just starting high school. Actually, they had four boys, but the oldest died of a drug overdose. After the divorce, Penny worked at the rectory as a secretary. Occasionally she would send me a Christmas card, and in one of them, she thought to tell me that Sister Patrice had died. She had lived to be ninety-two. "I said some awful things about the old coots when we were kids," Penny wrote. "And I guess I just now got around to feeling bad about it."

I wrote Penny back. "All those years ago, you were right about you and Mark, and I think you were right about Sister Patrice and Sister Mary Helena, too. It makes me happy to think they knew love, after all." I had her home address, but I sent it to the rectory, anyway.

It didn't surprise me that I never heard from Penny again.

HYENAS

Nothing had crystallized before then.

Before that, everything was conjecture. I had thought I felt that hum of interest, that invisible energy field of tension that somehow keeps you in the other's orbit. But I thought it was all coming from me. Maggie was coupled, though the failings of her relationship with Jan had been so well telegraphed and advertised through our group that she seemed nearly single. Or she seemed, rather, poised to leap, and we were all only watching to see where.

Why I was watching I wasn't sure. Later I figured out she reminded me of myself — a rebel caught up in some web of domesticity who was fine, content even, as long as she was kept from seeing the view from the moving train.

This was weeks later, though. She had driven a long way to meet us all — me and Cole and three other couples — but it seemed warranted, because we all knew she needed "to get away." It had nothing to do with me. Except almost immediately I wondered if it did. And then I wondered if I wondered that because, it hit me suddenly, I wanted it to. Have something to do with me, that is. Everything to do with me. That since the last time I saw her it was as if each day were a brick on my chest, the pressure negligible at first, and then, this day, I registered that I could barely breathe. She seemed to me wholly desirable: her thick, short hair the dark red of fall leaves, her smile somehow both aristocratic and prankish, her hands long-fingered and graceful. We did a slow-shoe dance of where to sit around the table, advancing casually — extremely important to look casual — stopping to shuffle when it looked as though someone else might wedge a chair between us, never meeting eyes. It was critical not to meet eyes.

Sure we *looked* at each other, but that's different. But Maggie was not a toucher, so it was impossible not to register that she touched me once, twice, three times while we sat there. The first two times were an open palm on my back, the second one more lingering than the first, as if measuring heat. Flat-palmed steadiness, I counted the beats. The third time was more skittish but it was on my thigh, two fingertips up high, close to the hip, with just a shade of pressure.

And yet, before that one look, I wasn't counting. I was barely noticing. Later, I realized I had been storing it all, and then what was random took shape, revealed motive, confirmed what was only suspected.

It blotted out everything, so that I don't remember at all what conversation came on either side. All I know is that I glanced up and found her eyes — those gorgeous hazel eyes — locked on mine, a phrase so overused we don't hear its authority. Because it *was* a lock; it took a kind of physical effort to pull my eyes away. And I did, almost instantly, because what I saw there was so unapologetic and unmistakable that it was as though I were passing into a flame.

Maggie was not a talker, she was not a confessor. She was efficient in conversation: if you asked her a question, her goal was always to impart the least amount of information possible. She never told you anything accidentally.

And yet, there was the whole story in that one look, a whole symphony of dare and desire, challenge and promise. It made my stomach kick over. I couldn't look at her the rest of the day. I was getting a stiff neck trying so hard not to look at her.

Later, in bed with Cole, I thought: what kind of woman does that? Tries to get in the middle of a couple? It was behavior that, in theory, I abhorred, I had railed against more times than I could count. But now it wasn't theory. It was Maggie. And it was me she wanted. Didn't I deserve that?

How quickly we make exceptions for ourselves. It happens so often and every time we're shocked: the priest who molests children or rapes a parishioner, the right wing politician who stars in his own S & M parties on weekends. We all think: My rules do not apply to me.

I started marking time differently. I said: Look how many years I've never cheated. I said: Look how many years it's been since I've been with someone new. I said: I've been faithful so long I was frightened by that look, the sheer bold invitation of it, the affirmation, the possibility.

And didn't I deserve that?

None of this I told Renee. Instead I told her only what was definite, indisputable: that Maggie had called me that night at work. Those facts alone made me appear blameless, at least at the outset. And I felt blameless. This is a trick of the psyche, of course: Cole simply dropped out of my field of vision. How can that be when you live with someone? It's easier that way, actually. You are part of each other's atmosphere, a thread in the fabric of your daily routine.

It was not my idea to throw Renee into the water that day in Provincetown, either. I knew how much she would hate it. Renee has no sense of humor for pranks. It was Maggie's idea, and like most of the ideas Maggie had since the night she seduced me, I found myself incapable of resisting. Why? Why. Probably because I had no idea what drew her to me, so I frantically followed every clue, to try to be more of what I thought she was responding to.

It was also Maggie's idea to come to

Provincetown with Cole and me. She claimed not to remember that I had told her we were going with Renee and Celia, the way we always do. She just said all the good places were booked already, and did I have any ideas? And the next thing I knew, I was saying there was a spare bedroom in our place. But she *wanted* me to offer that, wanted me to invite her. You could not really say it was my idea.

I didn't think about Jan either. I figured that was Maggie's problem. But I guess I thought Jan a little pale, a little undernourished for someone as robust as Maggie. It seemed the most natural thing in the world to me that Maggie would peel away from Jan, the way the bright green new shoots of a plant choke the life out of the older leaves in increments, until they seem like shadows and just fall away.

That first night, it didn't happen exactly the way I told Renee. *I* was the one who started crying, not Maggie. It's true that she began by talking about Jan, what was wrong with her and Jan, but everything she said sounded like me and Cole. That she couldn't bear having grown to feel like Jan's roommate, a fond old buddy, that she ached to feel like a lover again, to feel the urgency and out-of-breathness again, and the next thing I knew I was crying. She took me by the wrist and led me over to the couch, made me lie flat on my back with my head in her lap, while she pressed little circles into my temples. To calm me, she said. But it wasn't calming at all. A prickle swirled in my heels, my throat closed, and it felt like my ribcage was expanding. Her fingers — illicit, forbidden – along my forehead, across my eyebrows, down over the bridge of my nose, were as frankly sexual as anything that came later. That was my last chance, I knew, to pull myself up out of the quicksand and keep my life intact.

Afterward, on the way home, away from the drug of her touch, I felt wrecked, disassembled, mutinous, vile. But I also felt robbed, haggard with loss. Why? Not because Cole was lost for me, or I for her, though I felt instantly that was true. But because I realized that after your first great love, every passion that follows bears the bruise of guilt, the poison of betrayal. It is always second, always after failure. It is never the sweet first swallow. And I was so very, very sad about that.

Two months later, in mid-September, we went to a drive-through safari. We parked my car and exchanged it for one of the park's Jeeps, because, they told you in somber voices, they couldn't guarantee that some of the animals wouldn't charge the cars. I thought this was a clever cash-gouging scheme until we got stuck behind another Jeep for about ten minutes while two lions leisurely scratched their backs along the doors and bumpers, rocking the Jeep like a child's toy.

Maggie was taken with the zebras. And I could understand why. It was one thing to see them on your television screen, little domino-colored figurines, and another to see them twenty feet from your car. Most animals have the sense to be some soothing earth tone, and yet here were the zebras, with their cartoon-crazy design, dressed for a Manhattan party in black and white pajama stripes. Because where in nature would black and white stripes serve as camouflage?

Long range, Maggie explained to me, reading from the guide book we had bought. The stripes make them invisible at long range. They're actually horses, she said, in the way only a city girl can sound amazed by a nature fact. Of course, I was a city girl, too. I probably wouldn't have been able to tell you a zebra was a horse, either. "Who their natural enemies are," Maggie read. Among the most vicious: Hyenas, one of the most aggressive predators in the animal kingdom. Of which there were none on this safari for that very reason. They seem to take pleasure in destruction, and they leave little evidence behind. A pack of two dozen hyenas feasting on a 500-pound zebra will devour everything including bone, so that only blood in the dirt remains. In fact, she read, if a pair of hyena cubs are born together, one often kills and eats the other. This is possible because they are usually born with some teeth already in. And the females, for whatever reason — likely hormonal — are the most ferocious.

We moved onto other animals, but Maggie seemed to lose interest after that. Or really, she seemed to lose heart. I saw her glance worriedly several times in the direction of the zebras — until they did their striped disappearing act. Personally, I found the ostriches a goof. They glided up to the Jeep like huge cotton balls on toothpicks and stared like madmen through the window. They reminded me of a nightmare guest: someone hopelessly nerdy who was also over-friendly and impossible to ignore. Maggie did not share my amusement.

We were watching the antelopes and mountain goats clustered together like uncertain tourists when Maggie said, quietly, "I want you to leave Cole." The plains stretched so far in front of us outside the sealed air of our slow-moving Jeep that it was as if we weren't moving at all, as if time were holding its breath. Wanting her pressed forward from the inside, along every pore. If we stayed in this Jeep, on this safari road, the sun would never set, the day would never dim, and we would never stop wanting each other just as much as we did right now.

When I was a teenager, twenty years ago, I was unshakably certain that love was a constant, that it did not age, it did not have its youth, like a season, or its dusk, like a day. I did not know, twenty years ago, that you could stand in the same place twice, that hope would at some point never be pure, soiled with the stain of past regret or failure.

"Leave Cole?" I repeated. And yet, a current of something I hadn't felt in a long time – recklessness, adventure – moved along my limbs. Like when you're a kid and you realize for the first time that you might be able to feed your broccoli to the dog and get away with it. Delirium. Freedom.

"Yes, leave Cole," she said. What good was it going on like this? What was the point?

The point. The trouble was, I was tired of things having a point. I was finally just enjoying the *feeling* again. Now it had to have a point.

We were headed for the safari exit. You could tell because the scenery was thinning out to scrub, and there were no animals in sight. It was as if the hyenas had already been there, leaving the scene vacant after their desires were satiated.

"Take me home," Maggie said. "And don't call me again till you've left Cole."

It took me two weeks. Cole moved out the night I told her. Not with everything, of course, just enough to get through a day at a time without having to see me. She didn't tell me where she was going. But I guessed it was to Renee and Celia's place. That's where I would have gone, had it been Cole leaving me. They had a guest room; we'd stayed over plenty of times when we didn't feel like driving home.

I was nauseous the whole time I was telling her. To me it had the shock of violence, as if I were asking her to hold still while I hacked off her arm with a blunt instrument. It was so blatantly cruel, so obviously the wrong thing to be doing that second thoughts were not an issue. I knew while I was doing it that it was a mistake. Being without Cole would always be a mistake; there was no need to debate it. But Maggie had said I had to in order to be with her, and I could think of no way around that. I had run out of lies.

Maggie did not take my calls once during the whole ordeal. It was a tactic I saw the wisdom of: total deprivation forced me to hurry if I wanted even five minutes with her, let alone five years. I had become single-minded, suspicious. Everything was a plot to keep me from her. Even when Renee called, I spoke to her as though she were a heathen trying to keep a prophet from her holy mission. Renee said: I hope you don't think this is a vacation. Because if you let Cole stay away one more night, there's no turning back. She said: There's such a thing as killing hope. A few more days and you've lost her trust forever. And I actually stiffened at the other end of the phone. She was just jealous, close-minded, stuck.

I had liked driving the Jeep so much that day that I traded in my old car and bought one. Black, with leather bucket seats as deep as living-room recliners. We were parked on a quiet block a few blocks from Maggie's house when I told her: I had left Cole, we could be together. I had tonight in mind, specifically. Maggie's red-sneakered feet were up on my new dashboard; she was swaying her long, lean legs, bare in cut-off jeans, in time to the k.d. lang tape I had playing. Headlights from passing cars threw weird shadows across her face. I watched her, the memory of pleasure as sharp and real as the smell of new leather in my throat. I leaned over and kissed her, cupped the warm cave between her legs, traced the smooth, dark seam of her jeans till it went rough with moistness.

Then she stopped my hand. I've had two weeks, too, she said. Two weeks to think. And I've decided to give me and Jan another shot. She knows I'm out here with you now, telling you it's over.

I am the kind of person who lets puppies lord over me, because I can barely stand to raise my voice. I've never killed a bug, the crustiest, hairiest

41

among them, without agonizing for a moment about the great eternal nothingness I was sending it into.

And yet. And yet now I imagined slamming Maggie's head hard against the passenger window. The glass was the kind that would not break, the salesman had told me. It would shatter but stay intact. I imagined it now, Maggie's head making a round nest in the window, a mosaic of silver veins reaching out from the place where her skull collided with the glass, her face clenched in pain.

Get out, I said. I was aware of breathing in long, deep draughts. I did not look up. I heard the passenger door close, the sound of footsteps on the cement receding. I gave her time to get back to the house, time for her to feel relief, to imagine herself approaching the front door and telling Jan it was done. Then I turned the Jeep around, admiring its handling, and ran two stop signs to her house. I saw her getting ready to head up her driveway. I gunned the Jeep alongside her and pointed its black, blunt nose at the porch. I squeezed my eyes shut and floored the gas. I looked in time to see the wood splinter and fly skyward like sparks, with the requisite crunching and crashing sounds. I backed up and did it again, and saw Jan at the front door, pale, white-blonde Jan, her mouth moving in outrage, her arms swinging. The Jeep was in reverse when I saw Maggie bound up the front steps, her arms open protectively. I was back in drive, aiming again for the gutted porch, the steering wheel hot against my palms, when I thought, You don't know how lucky you are, Maggie. You have no idea.

TILL DEATH DO WE PART

Roseanne seems incongruous at her own wedding reception, a circumstance Renee might have thought was deliberate were it not so clear that Roseanne doesn't know it. It's as if Roseanne has preserved her childhood fantasy of what it would be like to be a bride, and superimposed it on the chaos of her current life. Her gown is delicately beaded with thousands of tiny faux pearls which make a light clacking sound whenever she scoops up the long train, and the sleeves reach down the backs of her hands in elegant points. Her hair is swept up in a swirl of dark loops; her eyes, more lushly lashed than Renee remembers, are stark against her porcelain face and rose-red lips. Renee has only recently read that lipstick originated as a way for whores to advertise that they would do blow jobs, and Renee hasn't been able to shake that impression yet.

The groom, however, is the hair in the soup, as Renee thinks of him. He is shorter than Roseanne by several inches, and broad across the belly in his brown tuxedo with velvet lapels. Long brown hair spills over his collar, and a dense beard and moustache camouflage his face. A sharp nose and almond-shaped eyes hint that he might be handsome underneath the growth. His slacks are tucked into black leather, silver-tipped and spurred boots; pewter skull and snake rings are immense on his fingers, squeezed past heavy knuckles.

Of all the things Renee has imagined Roseanne becoming — and she has allowed for many extravagant detours — the bride of a biker was not one of them. This is not something Renee can remark on because, though she feels confident that she has stopped actively criticizing, lampooning or otherwise judging Roseanne, Roseanne still narrows her eyes defensively, primed for insult, whenever she relays a new piece of information about her life to Renee. It's now more than fifteen years ago that they went to high school together and Renee, at least, is weary of the remnants of their adolescent relationship. But Roseanne seems not to have noticed; some of the high drama of their differences is alive and vital to her, a contest one of them still must win. If Renee falls back on old routines, like a standup comic resorting to jokes that got laughs before, it's only because she knows that without these, they are strangers. Familiar tension is a comfort when the alternative is apathy.

They are dancing the first dance, Roseanne and Dirk, to what must surely be the only ballad Aerosmith ever recorded. Dirk shuffles without rhythm, sometimes swinging them into a wide arc so he can grin hairily at several tablesful of his biker buddies, a group that, Renee has decided from her vantage point across the room, are not sufficiently bathed. Dirk has one hand on Roseanne's hip and the other is clenching her right hand into a prizefighter's fist, jerking it over their heads until Roseanne pulls free and nuzzles her head against Dirk's shoulder. They sway in relative calm for a few moments until Dirk releases her and walks off. The song is not completely over, and Roseanne is left blinking in the middle of the dance floor, like someone startled from sleep.

"The happy het couple," Celia murmurs to Renee so that the rest of their tablemates can't hear. Celia and Renee have been together five years and yet the invitation came addressed to Renee and "guest." Celia has told her to be grateful that she got invited with a guest at all, given that she is not married, but Renee insisted that if she were living with a man all these years, no one would have the gall to address him as "guest" instead of by his name. Or it might simply be that Roseanne's younger sister — a girl Renee once tutored in Catholic grammar school and who now has two out-of-wedlock children by the same local drug dealer — addressed the invitations and couldn't be expected to keep track of the details of the lives of her older sister's friends. Or it may be that Roseanne meant to communicate her lack of confidence in any relationship lasting long enough for a couple to still be together for the span of time it takes to accept a wedding invitation and then actually attend it. Or it may even have been to dodge her mother's scorn. Mrs. Amarato is a conspicuously non-fallen Catholic, and memories of her kitchen-counter sermons to Renee and Roseanne came flooding back when Renee had greeted the older woman earlier. She was like Roseanne's Dorian Gray; all the worry and distress Roseanne should have felt seemed to register only on Mrs. Amarato's face.

"Thanks for coming with me. I owe you one," Renee whispers back to Celia. Actually, she is more grateful than Celia knows. Lily, a mutual friend from high school who was supposed to be their tablemate had cancelled, claiming illness. Renee, disappointed into sullenness, has done her best to project a wall of silence around herself and Celia. And now, well into dessert, it's too late for any of their other tablemates — a misfit assortment of Roseanne's distant cousins and requisite neighbors — to strike up a conversation.

"Let me go say hello," Renee says, squeezing Celia's shoulder apologetically. She intercepts Roseanne as she is moving away from small talk with one table and heading toward another.

"Renee!" Roseanne says, gripping her friend's arm as if she is surprised to see her, as if it is some kind of coincidence that she is here. She presses a cheek, fragrant with foundation, close to Renee's. "Let me introduce you to Dirk. Where is the moron? Gone outside to get coked up with his friends," Roseanne says, answering her own question. "Come on. Let's go to the bathroom where we can talk. And then I can have a cigarette, too." She takes Renee by the wrist.

"You make a beautiful bride," Renee says, meaning it. Up close, there is a kind of glamour about her that Renee finds hard to believe is attributable only to makeup and the gown.

Roseanne snorts dismissively, breaking the spell.

The bathroom is empty. Roseanne leans against the door to keep everyone out. Occasionally someone tries to enter and she butts the door shut against them, bellowing, "Bride in here. Come back later."

Roseanne was not one of the ones Renee had been in love with. Renee had spent the first two years of high school falling in love with someone else and the second two years trying to get over her. There hadn't been time for much else, and she had been stunned to discover that Roseanne had been jealously, angrily, waiting for Renee to take her affection seriously.

"Can you believe I did it, finally? Can you believe I got *him* to?" Roseanne asks, flexing her nostrils with a vigorous inhale. She holds the cigarette with the tips of her fingers, like a joint.

"No, I can't believe it, really," Renee says. "How'd it happen?"

"I left him. I meant it, it wasn't a ploy. I was really out of there. He hounded me for two months to come back, said he'd marry me, and he did."

"What does it mean, a biker marriage?" Renee asks. Because she knows that Dirk met Roseanne at a

47

bar where she was a topless dancer. In those days, she would sometimes arrange to meet men in their cars after her shift, sometimes for "tips," sometimes just because she was bored or curious or horny.

"Same thing it means to everyone else," Roseanne says, halfway into another deep inhale. "That you don't fuck around. That you give a shit."

"It sounds so romantic when you put it that way." Renee's solo laugh ricochets off the pale pink tile walls. Her temples go moist. She sees that Roseanne decides she has been mocked again, but for now she doesn't sulk.

"So what's your deal? Are you and Celia going to have some kind of ceremony? Now that you're living together?"

"No, I don't think so."

Roseanne nods sympathetically but Renee knows she doesn't, couldn't understand. Weddings make Renee sarcastic. It's like marital apartheid: straights and gays live essentially the same lives but only straights get the rights and protections of state and society. She doesn't keep this observation from Roseanne to spare her a lesson in gay politics, but because Roseanne is so far from experiencing any of her own circumstances as anything but serendipity that the explanation would only make her think Renee paranoid and strident.

What unsettles Renee now is to think that for Roseanne, their affair — which, when they finally had it, was short-lived, full of histrionics and ambivalence on both their parts for different reasons — was just the first in a series of outrageous stunts and bizarre activities Roseanne dabbled in, after which she just moved on, as easily as changing a channel that didn't suit.

"I guess our parents didn't imagine either of us turning out the way we did — although at least my mother did get a son-in-law."

"That's true. He *is* male," Renee says, perhaps a bit too sharply. She tries now to soften her tone, adopt a generous attitude. "So what will you do now, the two of you?"

"Dirk wants to make his jewelry full-time. It would mean traveling a lot to do the shows. He made everything he's wearing, you know."

Renee is unprepared for the edge of pride in Roseanne's voice. The three of them — Renee, Roseanne, and the absent Lily — get together for only a few lunches a year now, and maybe a few phone calls in between, but Roseanne was always so ready with stories of Dirk's betrayals and insensitivities that Renee is amazed that Roseanne can still be stirred to tenderness toward him. Women — and this seemed true whether they took male or female lovers — appeared to have a huge capacity for forgiveness. Renee considers herself an exception. She knows she is a grudge-keeper, a harsh judge, but she feels she makes up for this with strenuous loyalty once she decides someone is trustworthy.

"And what about you?" Renee asks, disturbed that Dirk's plans seem to be the answer for both of them.

"Well, if we travel, I'll have to quit. I can temp wherever we are," Roseanne says. She has evidently done well at the Manhattan law firm where she is a secretary, though Renee has always wondered what the Oxford-shirted attorneys make of Roseanne's tattoos and five-earringed ears. She suspects that they are partly titillated, that they think of her as local color.

"I'm glad you came," Roseanne says, shy, the gruff biker woman pose gone. Now she is the princess again with the found shoe, a glimmering and hopeful future ahead of her. "I gotta knock these things off," she continues, drowning her cigarette under the faucet before tossing it into the aluminum trash dispenser in the wall. "I get out of breath real easy these days. And I think they kill my appetite. Dirk wants to fatten me up. He hates it when I lose a few pounds." She noisily fluffs her shimmering gown around her.

"Have you been dieting?" Renee asks, incredulous, because Roseanne has always been lean, even past the age when such a thing came naturally for all of them.

"No, for the first time. And I'm losing weight, anyway."

A clammy heat makes Renee's ears glow and a spiral of fear cycles down to her knees and feet, making them leaden and tingly. "Have you been to a doctor?" she manages.

"Yeah, after a funny rash I had a few months ago. Stop *looking* at me like that. It was just a rash. People get rashes. I've been tested. We both have. I'm not stupid. We're fine, all clear."

Roseanne lights another cigarette and resumes her post at the door. Renee sees that she no longer knows Roseanne well enough to tell if she is lying about any part of it. She wonders if she's bluffing, if she's never mentioned these symptoms to anyone else before and needs now to gauge if her fear is warranted.

"Well, as long as you've been to a doctor," Renee says, working to keep the wobble of doubt out of her voice. Someone thumps vigorously at the door and Roseanne warns them away.

"It's me," calls Mrs. Amarato. "Let me in, I gotta pee."

The gray woman enters, creating more commotion than Renee would have thought possible for one person. She splashes and shouts, makes faces at herself in the mirror, fires questions at Renee: Did she like the food? Did she meet Dirk? How were her parents, her job? Renee remembers Roseanne telling her once that her mother didn't trust anyone who couldn't look her in the eye. Since then, Renee has made it a point to bore into Mrs. Amarato's eyes with her own, in a way that now seems to unnerve the older woman. Renee thinks this is what keeps her from asking if she is seeing any nice young men.

Roseanne rolls her eyes when her mother is finally behind a stall, and motions to Renee to follow her out. The band has started up again.

Renee remembers them in Roseanne's parents' bed together: the sheets were foreign and adult, the pillows needed to be pried from starched, ruffled shams. Renee had been the experienced one, the one who already knew what it was like to touch another girl. Roseanne was content to have Renee be the wise and brave one always, and this adventure was no exception. It was, Renee realizes now, a powerful aphrodisiac at seventeen, when she was still figuring out what it meant to be a woman who loved women.

From the start, Renee knew they had not been meant for each other; they had been both friends and strangers for too long. Strangers because Roseanne had always dated boys, even while Renee was turning herself inside out over the first girl she had fallen in love with. And it was an alien and terrifying thing to feel so sure of incompatibility with Roseanne after having been so certain of destiny in her first love. Renee felt guilty about that, and made up for it by being a curious and energetic lover. She had kissed Roseanne in places she hadn't had the courage to with her first lover, had pressed herself inside and discovered, blindly, a dark and textured landscape rigged with pleasures all around. Roseanne, stunned and grateful, would dart up from bed afterward and bring back food — soft cheeses and olives, chocolate and grapes. She would let Renee choose the albums; she would graze her fingertips slowly over Renee's scalp in the way she knew mesmerized her.

Their affair had started just a few weeks before graduation; in a perverse twist, Renee was going to the prom with a boy she knew expected nothing of her, but Roseanne was not going at all. By then, Roseanne seemed to want something raw and reckless that the senior boys were unable to comprehend. For that moment in time, Roseanne was suspended between her present and her own potential, with no resources to bridge the gap. Renee knew she was some kind of bridge, but Roseanne kissed her as though she were forever.

They were expecting no one this one night; Roseanne's parents were at a party upstate and had arranged to stay over at a nearby couple's house. So when the front door flew open, and they heard a man's voice, panicky, yelling, "Roseanne! Rose*anne*!" Renee felt her body go cold as stone.

"It's my uncle — get some *clothes* on!" Roseanne had commanded, but he was up the stairs before they were completely dressed. And yet he was blind with his purpose, hugging himself, wailing. "Oh, honey, your daddy, it's your daddy." Something about traveling from the supper club to the house, a drunk driver, her mother was unscathed, but her daddy. . . . Roseanne had turned, shirtless, and clung to Renee like a widow; Renee had wished the man, who looked unbearably like Roseanne's father, would leave. Instead he hugged his elbows and whimpered, paced the room, had no plan.

It was Roseanne's father, after all, who had been her ally, the good cop to her mother's bad. After his death, Roseanne seemed flattened by grief, determined to prove that if fate or God or the universe had been so intent on screwing up her life, she would go it one better. And she did, in spectacularly heavy-handed ways.

Renee had always felt responsible. She had had her moment to save Roseanne, or to at least retrieve her from the worst, and she couldn't or didn't or wouldn't. If she had been in love, it would have been different. It would have been different for them both.

* * * * *

53

Celia is a natural, sensual dancer, and Renee forgets her own self-consciousness, caught up in watching Celia, who is dazzling tonight in her red dress and her blonde curls piled high. When she and Renee finish out a song, one of the bikers intercepts and asks Celia for the next dance. Renee can tell by Celia's glance that she doesn't mind, that she thinks it will be less complicated than refusing, but that she won't do it if Renee insists. Renee retreats to the table, and for a second remembers how she felt at high school dances when an approaching boy reminded her that, for most of them, the girls danced together only by default. The biker is a grizzled example of the alternative, but watching them, Renee tries to imagine, as she sometimes does, what her life would have been like as a married woman, full of the simplicity of expectations fulfilled. If there is penis envy at all, this is it: she sometimes longs to be able to bring a man home to her parents, to have them see her as they imagined her from the time of her infancy, at the side of some man with an aggressive, masculine profile, a protective arm around her waist. But she has grown so used to her badge of difference, of "other," that she wonders now — if she and Celia were truly and totally accepted everywhere — whether part of her identity would be lost. When the song ends and the biker walks off, Renee feels tension she didn't even know was there ease out of her shoulders.

"What was he saying to you?" Renee asks before Celia even makes contact with her chair again.

"He asked if I would have his children. Sons only. Daughters we bury out back."

"Very funny. Well, actually not. It's probably not far from the truth."

"Relax." Celia puts an arm around Renee's shoulders briefly, and Renee tries not to flinch. She still has to remind herself occasionally that a certain amount of physical contact between women passes without suspicion. In fact, not recognizing that from out of her haze of paranoia was what got her into trouble in college. Every cheerful hug was suspect; she worried sweatily if every other girl was coming on to her.

People are marching up to the dessert table for the Viennese hour with barely restrained impatience. The spread of pastel-colored cakes and pastries seems to ignite a kind of fever in the room. Renee, who is famous among her friends for her appetite for sweets, finds herself with no interest.

Celia has brought back two small plates towering with a smorgasbord of desserts. Renee smiles, knowing that Celia considers her refusal of dessert a temporary lapse that will be easily conquered. For Celia's sake, and as a show of gratitude, Renee picks at an enormous brownie, but the longer she watches Roseanne sitting at the dais alone, scanning the doorways for a sign of Dirk's return, the more the sweets turn to straw in her mouth.

Celia squeezes Renee's knee under the table. "Don't worry. He's just being a macho jerk in front of his friends. He's probably perfectly decent to her when they're alone."

"So you think it's obvious to everyone, then?" Renee asks, glancing around the room, with its identical tables of dressed up men and women, boy-girl, boy-girl, nearly without exception.

"Well, no one's gotten to bang their glasses with their forks much and watch the newlyweds kiss. I imagine that must be a disappointment."

Renee pushes away from the table before Celia can protest, before she can reasonably point out that this is really none of her business. "I'll be right back."

The parking lot is poorly lit and all Renee can see are car roofs shiny in the streetlights. She walks out to the road but there are no side streets, only highway, and no sign of any possible hideaway for a rude groom and his rowdy friends. Without a plan, she begins to walk up and down the aisles of parked cars, moving quickly to cheat the October night's chill.

If she finds him, she doesn't know if she will be nonchalant and say something about the expensive desserts he is missing, or if she will give in to her growing anger and allow herself the satisfaction of berating him for abandoning his bride at his own wedding.

It's only shadows that catch her eye and draw her close to an old Cadillac near the fence. Music rises up from it faintly like a scent. There are silhouettes in the darkness of the back seat, shadows against shadows, pieces of the night moving according to their own rhythm. Something about the car frightens her but she presses forward with the dread of someone investigating a loud noise in a dark empty house. Finally she is close enough to see two men in the back seat, one crouched on the floor between the other man's legs, his long brown hair falling forward over the other's bare thighs. The one seated has his head thrown back, wincing with pleasure; the one on the floor is gripping the front of the seat for balance. Renee can see the skull and snake rings glinting on his pudgy fingers as he pushes forward, deeper into the other man's shadows.

Renee trips as she runs back to the reception hall, kicking herself in the back of the ankle and going down hard on her left knee. Blood squeezes in neat stripes through her shredded stocking. Her knee feels simultaneously numb and fiery, but it's pain she recognizes, at least, pain she has had experience with. She will go in and ask Roseanne to help her clean it, to rummage for Band-Aids, maybe even find a fresh pair of pantyhose carried by a conscientious bridesmaid. All those details will keep her occupied, will help distract her, Renee hopes, for a little while longer.

HELL HATH NO WRATH

I knew as early as the summer that Edie was involved with someone else. I mean, I wasn't sure she was actually sleeping with someone else. In fact, I was pretty sure she *wasn't,* even though that turned out not to be true. But I could tell she was in love with another woman.

The whole time we were together, I always suspected there was some quiet center, some ultimate private place, where she felt things she would never say. I guess we both had one. Like, for instance, even though the sex between us had become sporadic and uninspired, we never said this aloud; we said that we loved each other like crazy and that was the only thing that mattered.

I *knew* Edie, so when I confronted her and she denied it, it was gratuitous a double blow. Because then she was lying to my face. I don't know why that was somehow worse — that she thought she could get away with lying to my face. Maybe because way deep down, in my own quiet center, I could imagine wanting to sleep with another woman, imagine wanting to part a new woman's thighs and feel that pounding ache all up and down from your lips to your toes, like you'd die if you don't have her. Maybe I could have figured out a way to forgive her that. But I couldn't forgive her lying.

After I left Edie the night she told me about Maggie, I stayed with Renee and Celia for a month and a half. It was an outrageous imposition — I knew it, we all knew it, but I was as incapable of going out to look for a new place to live as I was to turn my skin inside out. Finally, it was Celia who gently told me one morning that she had lined up a string of apartments for me to see; I put down a deposit for the third one we looked at without even debating its merits. I had so little energy and interest that I'd have taken the first one if that hadn't seemed reckless.

I realized after I moved out of Renee and Celia's place that being on my own was for the best. Because Renee and Celia got more cozy with each other once I was there — I was like the town leper who made you so goddamn down-to-your-toes grateful that you've got your health. And I could tell they really didn't know how to act with me — we had gotten so used to an energy field of four that we couldn't seem to carry on a three-way conversation.

The worst part was, no one could really comfort me. It's the most desolate feeling in the world when the person you most naturally turn to to soothe you, the one you've always confided your humiliations and fears and terrors to, is the one who inflicts the worst wound. It's like one of those movies where the star turns out to have an evil twin. I really didn't recognize her, the night she told me about Maggie, about choosing Maggie. I was thinking, Where's Edie? Where'd they take *Edie*? I gotta tell Edie this horrible thing that just happened to me. She'll know what to do.

After I moved into my own place, silence set in. It was a pore-deep silence, a mausoleum-style silence that, after a while, I became reluctant to break. I was loath to turn on the TV or radio; I cooked as quietly as possible. I resented it when the phone rang, and was offended and embarrassed by the sound of my own voice. When Edie and I lived together, the house was always full of the low-grade noise of a life together — the shouting to each other from room to room, the clatter of a meal prepared and consumed side-by-side, the maintenance of a social life and shopping excursions and bill-paying and repair-making all done on the phone. It was as if I began to feel I could avoid being reminded of all this purposeful sound if I just stayed very quiet. Then quiet would come to seem normal, status quo. Except at night I would make a racket crying myself to sleep, crying till my skull vibrated and my nose felt swollen and my eyes were so hot I needed ice pressed against the lids. And I never turned out the lights: I kept them blaring in every room, even the bedroom, all through the night. I had timers set to turn them out at daybreak.

After a while, I started spending my evenings in malls. There were plenty in New Jersey — huge, cavernous, ear-splitting places with enough color and motion to make you dizzy. They were more like mini-cities, except they were better because they were climate-controlled and you only spent money, never busted your hump earning it. I bought sweatpants and soft pretzels, CDs and sneakers, bath towels and lithographs.

Eventually I bought a puppy.

It was a mistake, I knew it, even as they were handing me the bony, wriggling springer body, newly baby-powdered and leashed. It's nearly impossible to housebreak a puppy when you work 10-hour days, and I didn't have a backyard or a basement run. But such was the depth of my pathos that I was willing to compound my practical problems in exchange for the kind of ecstatic, unconditional love that dogs give. And in fact Beatrice was the model puppy — or at least had the model bladder — because she seemed to catch on to the domestic house-breaking thing effortlessly. And having her meant there was no longer that black-hole of despair when I came home from work at night. There would be Beatrice, her happiness at seeing me as innocent and uncomplicated as sweet tea on a cold night. And in the morning, when I got up, she would get up with me, pressing her body to the floor in a grateful stretch, rubbing away the doggie dreams in her eyes against my ankle. Beatrice saved me money on therapy and she and I became a team.

But eventually even Beatrice was not enough. I had some coiled, hot-angry thing in me that I shielded even from her. So that's when I started with the clippings. They were always small stories, sometimes only a who-what-where-when paragraph, tucked into the corners of the newspaper. And I mean the corners, because I read a respectable, staid newspaper, not the gaudy tabloids whistling and winking from the supermarket racks. Once I started paying attention, it didn't take long for them to accumulate: *19 Year Old Man Sets Fire To Salons That Gave Him Bad Haircuts*, out of Los Angeles; *Two Men, Angry Over Last Call, Cut Bar In Half With Chain Saw*, from Torrington, Connecticut; *300 Pound Woman Sits On Husband During Argument, Crushes Him To Death*, dateline Milwaukee. It was exhilarating to read about people who were spectacularly bad sports, who let their rage over a perceived injustice – no matter how slight – lead them to such desperate and dramatic revenge.

And I did not want to be well-behaved in my misery. I did not want to be one of those women who "take it well." I wanted to blow up Edie's parakeets, if only she had them. I wanted to smear her entire wardrobe with Vaseline. I wanted to merge her credit rating with someone the IRS had on their Most Wanted list. And I wanted to never forgive her, even if that cancelled out my other wish: To have her back, wholly and completely, forever.

Maybe it's quaint, the idea of monogamy. But there really isn't a better system. Because here's the central paradox: Everybody wants to cheat but nobody wants to be cheated on. So you lie for a while to bridge that reality gap. I knew that, Edie knew that, but it was always something other women did to each other. Besides, we were living together five years — you're past the point where you worry every time she meets a new woman at a party, because the two of you are no longer like truly separate people. You're more like a new organism, a seesaw that's lopsided when the other half is missing. I was not one of those women who found any comfort in blaming the interloper: I blamed Edie a hundred and ten percent — no, two hundred percent, enough for both of them. Because what did I care about what Maggie did? None of it would have come to anything if Edie hadn't cooperated. And Edie was the one who loved me, who said she loved me. It was like some Biblical rage, some tribal vengeance that makes your skin glow; you can set fires with just the touch of a fingertip.

And yet, there was this ridiculous thing going on at the same time: I still loved her. How could I not? The betrayal sometimes seemed like it voided everything that came before, everything about our love. And other times, it seemed like an isolated aberration, some freaky quirk of temptation and circumstance that would be best overlooked, like a burp in an elegant restaurant. I'd think about the way she said goodbye that night when I moved out, as

63

sweet and tender as any leave-taking before, when I'd be heading off on a trip without her, or she without me, the same embrace we'd given in a crowded airport or on the doorstep, the same automatic check to make sure that the other had her scarf or briefcase or tickets. The same concern, the same goodbye kiss, the same little squeeze of tears. Because a part of us did still love each other the same exact way, with the same exact hope that we'd have our whole lives, whatever they were to be, to spend with each other.

Whenever I felt myself start to soften, I'd remember a couple of things: The fact that she was lying to me for so long, sleeping in our bed, eating at our breakfast table, when she'd shared these same intimacies with another woman. And the other thing I remembered was the way she looked at me when I asked her if she really thought she loved Maggie as much as she loved me. "I love her in a different way," she said. And that's the line that made me sick, set me packing. Because there is no different way. There is only one way.

25 Year Old Man Shoots Arrow Into Heart Of Friend After Fight Over Monopoly Game Rules, out of Doylestown, Pennsylvania. I clipped and clipped and clipped, and regretted bitterly that I did not have the courage to give in to my worst instincts.

I was not expecting a Jeep that November morning, so I didn't move from the front door when I saw it stop. It wasn't until the driver honked that I looked more closely and saw it was Edie.

"You didn't tell me you got a new car," I said, stepping up into it. "Or is it new? It looks a little roughed up." I didn't like its square-cornered efficiency, its surrealistic vantage several feet over the tops of mere cars.

"Yeah, it's new. Guess I forgot to tell you. In all the excitement." She smiled like a timid child meeting a stranger, uncertain whether she has encountered friend or foe. "Thanks for meeting me," she said into the sideview mirror as she pulled into traffic.

I was irritated by her smile and her casual thanks; it was too familiar, too comfortable, for my tastes. Old lovers cannot fight with the kind of sweeping, sterile hostility that strangers or even new lovers can. People say that when you know someone a long time, you can be more cruel, but it's not true. You can't call someone you've loved for five years a conniving, unfeeling bitch — not with any credibility, anyway, not with the authority of just having discovered it — because then what does that say about your judgment all those years? Every punch you throw has its "umph" broken by all the kisses that came before. Every kick and slap declares itself merely the flip side of past caresses.

"You're not talking to me?" Edie asked.

I examined her in silence. She had gained some weight, enough that it showed in her face, but she had a smart new haircut that was fuller, softer. "I'm not the one with something to say. You're the one who wanted to talk."

She nodded with more emphasis, I thought, than necessary. I knew she was getting the feeling that this was not going to be as easy as she thought. But now I had to get across the message that it was impossible.

"I thought we'd go have a bite somewhere, but —" She glanced over at me — "maybe you don't feel up to eating?"

"Not especially."

"Why don't we just talk here in the Jeep, then? I'll pull over somewhere."

I said nothing. I wanted her to feel ridiculous, awkward, unwelcome. She was the one who had insisted we see each other in person.

She started scanning but she knew the neighborhood well enough to know that there weren't any cozy parks or waterfront overlooks, at least nothing close enough that the ride there would be easy to make in silence or strained half-sentences. She made a left across the on-coming traffic lane into a construction site. The work had been stalled, no doubt due to some investor with cold feet. Several towering pyramids of possibly toxic New Jersey soil were clustered around us, pointing dumbly at the winter-white sky.

Edie turned off the car, keeping the key cocked just enough so the radio stayed on. Some harpsichord-sounding instrumental was on. She didn't look at me; she just kept kneading the top of the steering wheel with both palms. I noticed she was wearing our matching five-year ring. I wondered if she had noticed that I was not.

"What I really wanted . . . the thing I really only . . . I mean, I wanted to tell you that it didn't work out with Maggie and me." She didn't take her eyes off the steering wheel. She was hunched over it now, gripping it hard.

I had heard this, or actually Renee had, and told me. The only surprising thing was Edie's timing: They had actually broken up in September. It was now November.

"Well, say something," she said.

"I was just thinking that if things *had* worked out, you and I would not be sitting here having this conversation. And that you probably don't understand that that's exactly why this conversation is so repulsive to me."

"It was a mistake."

"Which part?" I dead-panned.

"Everything. Everything but us."

"Easy to say now."

"No, not easy. Harder than you'll know." Color rose in her cheeks.

I shook my head, looked out the window at the piles of dirt, tall as buildings. The soil was not, as it appeared from the road, one uniform color. Several shades of brown swirled through it, and its damp, primitive smell seemed to seep through the sealed windows into my throat. "What have you been doing for the two months since it happened? Trying to patch things up with her?"

"Of course not," she said slowly, injured-sounding, insulted. "Of *course* not. I mean, I . . . I was terrified to call you. I couldn't face you. I couldn't think of a thing to say that would make any sense. My worst nightmare was that you wouldn't . . . that. . . . I mean, every day I got up and tried to think of a way to explain – no, not explain, just a way to say something that would make you not shut me out forever. To say how stupid I was, how sorry . . ."

She covered her face with her hands and began to cry, a wounded, inconsolable sound. I studied her closely in her familiar brown leather bomber jacket, strained for a whiff of the spicy perfume she always wore. The physical fact of her seemed miraculous, shockingly concrete, since these last few months she had existed only in my imagination. Part of me craved contact with her skin, with her body and the heat of it, but I knew it wasn't possible, wasn't allowed.

"I used to think," Edie said, dragging her hand across one wet eye and cheek, "that out there, from the time you were born, there was one special person destined just for you. And the trick was just finding and recognizing that person."

There were few things you didn't know about a person after five years, few things that weren't confessed over one of a thousand meals or during one of a thousand car rides. I knew all about Edie's theories of romance. And now I knew how they were different from the practice.

"I guess I'm embarrassed that I just now figured out that that isn't true," she said. "You know?"

I shook my head.

"I mean," she said, "that the way it really is is that you try to hook up with someone who cares about the same things you do, who sees the world something of the same way you see it, and from there you work at it. That there's no white doves in a handkerchief involved. That the love is in the

68

work." She looked over at me, her nostrils ringed red and her lips splotchy.

"And that's what you just now figured out?"

"I know it does no good to apologize for Maggie." She was back at the steering wheel, making it squeak in her hands. "I know you can't forgive that. I mean, I wouldn't. I couldn't, I admit it."

"You thought maybe if you were having to work so hard at us, it couldn't be destiny," I said. "Then when it felt like it was coming easy, that must have been true love."

"I forgot . . . I forgot how easy everything is in the beginning."

"Everything doesn't have to be so hard later on, either. If it was that hard for you, maybe we *were* all wrong."

"No! I didn't mean it was hard. I just meant it wasn't . . ."

"Like it was at the beginning?" I was staring her down. "That's why we have different words for these things. The beginning. The middle." I paused. "And the end."

She smiled slowly, an invitation, asking me to let this be only a word game, a reprimand she would gratefully submit to if it meant I planned to forgive her eventually. She wanted us to share the slow release of a laugh, the closest thing we'd have had to our old intimacy since I got in the car. And it had to be right now, at this moment when she had turned her belly up and waited. If we could not agree on what things could be made light of, then it was hopeless. I stayed solemn and looked away.

"I'm sorry, I. . . . Maybe I shouldn't have come. Maybe two months wasn't enough to. . . ." She turned the ignition key, devoted all her attention to turning us around. "I think I'm going to get rid of this Jeep," she said, when we were back on the road, returning to my apartment. "It doesn't seem to agree with me."

"Yes, it could be the Jeep," I said. We said nothing during the short ride back. The silence was like a presence, a stranger who sits too close and stares. When she pulled to the curb, I stepped down, but didn't close the door.

"You're okay, though? Your apartment is okay?" She was stalling, I knew, trying to hatch another strategy in these last few moments, maybe just wear me down by seeming inevitable, familiar.

"Uh-huh. Good enough. I have a dog. Maybe you'll meet her sometime."

"Yeah. Well. Sometime I'd like that." She smiled slightly, wringing her hands around the steering wheel again, as if it were stubborn putty.

"By the way," I said, "I hope someday you get back to believing the part about the white doves and the handkerchief. I think you did five years ago. I think I did, too." I pushed the passenger door, heard its airtight aluminum clap.

Through the window, she looked panicked. Her mouth opened and I saw her lean across the passenger seat to grope for the door, to push it forcefully away from her.

I waved and turned away, heading up the stairs before I could be convinced.

PARTY LINES

Diner chicken soup was one of the few things that could soothe Renee's nerves on days like this, when the cover story came in not just late but bad, and the writer enclosed a note saying he was leaving town and wouldn't be reachable for three weeks. That alone wouldn't have been so bad, but the day after tomorrow, she'd just learned by memo, all the department heads were to meet with the editor-in-chief, who wanted to discuss why newsstand sales were down for the last month. And, Renee had begun to suspect, her best staff reporter might be interviewing for another job.

"Uh oh, it's a bowl, not just a cup day, I see," Micki said, grinding out her cigarette as the waiter put her club sandwich down.

Renee morosely ticked off the day's disasters, trying to speak loudly enough over the crash and clatter of the diner, but not so loudly that anyone else who was here from the office but not within view would overhear.

"Yeah, we heard about that meeting, too," Micki said. "Greg's already talking about a re-design — even though we haven't even worked all the bugs out of the *last* re-design."

"Tell Greg to keep his color bars to himself for a while," Renee said. "You notice that only editorial — not the art department — is invited to the public lashing."

"Well, you tell Owen for me to stop picking on edit. You guys have been doing nothing but a great job. Tell him to go kick some butts on the sales staff for a change."

Renee smiled grudgingly. She was honing her bad mood the way you'd sharpen a weapon before battle; she didn't really want anyone to dull her edge. And yet Micki — part college-dorm buddy, part avenger of schoolyard bullies — was always able to lighten her mood. Renee knew what it was like to work in an office without a single friend or ally, and she never wanted to repeat that torment again. She counted Micki on her short list of things that made her job bearable during the worst times. In some ways, she was her most important daytime relationship; she was grateful more than once that Micki wasn't gay and that the bond had never been complicated by a crush. And yet she knew the friendship was particular only to work, even only to this job; in another setting, it would die like a plant repotted in inhospitable soil.

"Who do you think Rick's interviewing with?" Micki asked.

"Probably *Angle,* who else?" Renee said. *Angle* was a new monthly covering the city, heavy on lifestyle. Even though *Pulse* covered just "the business of New York" as its extended logo described, there was fear that circulation and advertising could be hurt. And *Angle* had the advantage of the backing of a huge publishing conglomerate.

"I'm surprised they haven't called you yet," Micki said.

"Nah. They can't raid from the senior staff — we're too associated with the competition, with the old guard they're trying to trounce. But they want the talented juniors so they can claim to have taken the spark plugs away. And they give them big promotions in exchange for state secrets."

"Nasty."

"I've done it myself when I worked on a start-up," Renee said. "I never thought I'd be part of the old guard someplace."

"I never thought the next big birthday I'd be dreading would be forty, either, so welcome to Life Goes On," Micki said, pulling at the top of her dark curly hair, partly, Renee knew, to keep it fluffy, but partly just out of nervous habit. Micki turned sideways in her chair, leaned her back against the faux brick wall, and lit another cigarette. "Do anything fun this weekend?" she asked, crossing her legs. Renee could see her black stirrup pants disappear into red suede flats.

Renee crumpled her napkin and watched the dessert rotary as it turned; she was considering whether this was a full-fledged chocolate cheesecake-in-the-afternoon kind of misery. She decided against it; eating dessert in front of most straight women, who looked on with the longing of an orphan watching an Osmond Family special, was just no fun. "We took in a movie, dinner with friends. And Celia's got it in her head now that maybe she'd like to trade the apartment for a house, so we went neighborhood window-shopping."

Renee watched as Micki nodded through a cloud of smoke. Though they'd been buddies for a year, they'd talked about Renee's private life — and at work it *was* mostly private, beyond the simple fact of it — only in the last few months. It was the usual pattern: Renee had had to wait until she was sure Micki had figured it out, so that the announcement was old news and Micki didn't have to work through her disorientation and discomfort right there across the lunch table. She'd had to endure, without comment, such disclaimers as "I don't care at all" and "It doesn't matter to me one bit who you sleep with" and pretend that these communicated great tolerance — as if tolerance was even what was called for. Try passing off those lines as a show of support to a straight co-worker who'd just gotten engaged, Renee'd complained to Celia later. Fortunately, she hadn't begun to expect more than the usual from Micki, so she hadn't been disappointed the way she'd been other times at earlier jobs with other friends. At least

Micki hadn't told her, in exchange, some tale of sudden death or treachery the way other straight friends had when she'd told them, as if they thought the point of the conversation was to confide past traumas.

"How about you?" Renee asked, when she saw that Micki could think of no follow-up question.

"John and I went to a wedding," Micki said, her voice shaded with regret and envy. She and her boyfriend had been living together close to seven years — if boyfriend was the right word for a forty-four-year-old man with two college-age kids from a first marriage. Renee understood a straight woman's pain over that one: Seven years was long enough for a man to start to be seriously bored, even though, for a woman who wants to be married, the real relationship hasn't even begun yet.

"He's a shit, really, most of the time," Micki said. Micki'd tried, more than once, to draw Renee into a heated male-bashing exchange, no doubt assuming that, as a lesbian, Renee would warm to the subject. When Renee didn't respond, she saw that Micki didn't understand that Renee had far less reason to resent straight men for anything, given that Renee's life hummed along complete without a single one in it, if you didn't count her father and the president.

It was just her dark mood that was making her hypersensitive to Micki's failings today, Renee thought, chiding herself. None of this stuff mattered at work, anyway. The important thing was that Micki was her reality check, her confidence booster, her sounding board, when it came to office crises. And now she had more than a few to return to.

"Come on, let's get back before they give our jobs away," Renee said, pushing away from the table, bracing herself for the bustle of traffic to the cashier.

"Nah," Micki said. "We'll never get that lucky."

Though she'd been at lunch only forty-five minutes, there was a little stack of messages left on her desk by the department secretary. Several were from writers she didn't have the energy to hand-hold just then. Two were from industry sources promising good leads on stories — which translated into wanting coverage of their companies and Renee's having to take them to an expensive lunch, complete with her best suit and most uncomfortable pumps, to get a promise of an exclusive out of them. And one was from Celia ("not important," the message said), which meant she'd probably just wanted to say hi. Renee figured it took the secretaries about two months to suspect, and the third month to be sure. But none of them had ever freaked out on her; they treated Celia's calls with the same friendly deference they did the other editors' husbands and wives. And Renee didn't mind the exposure: She considered it a chance to educate people she'd never have confided in otherwise. She liked to imagine them — mostly kids right out of college fantasizing about taking her job one day — going back to their buddies from school and saying, Hey, guess what? My boss is a dyke, but you know what? You'd *never* know.

On her chair was a stiff white envelope; she recognized the handwriting as belonging to the editor-in-chief's secretary. It was an invitation to a formal cocktail party honoring the companies listed by *Pulse* in this month's Christmas issue as the ones who gave the most back to the city. Renee had put in more weeks of late nights on the project than she cared to remember; she'd come to associate all the companies with the smell of wonton soup and shrimp fried rice, which was what she was invariably wolfing down at eight o'clock at night as she worked on manuscripts. She called down to Owen's office and told his secretary to count her in at the party. Celia would be sulky over another solo dinner thanks to the project, but Renee knew the event wasn't exactly optional.

"Well, I guess this will be John's debut," Micki said to Renee as she stood in the doorway, shrugging into her blazer, clearly ready to leave for the night.

"What will be?" Renee jumped slightly at Micki's voice; she had been absorbed in an on-screen edit of the wretched cover story.

"The party. The Companies Who Give Back shindig."

"John's going? You lost me."

"Who else would I bring, silly?"

"I didn't think we could bring anyone."

"You're invited with a guest. Look at your invitation." Micki stepped into Renee's office, scanning her desk top. Finding her invitation, she snapped it up. "Huh. Just your name." She shook out the envelope, turned everything over a few times, frowning all the while. "Phyllis must have made a mistake. Call her back."

"No, no mistake," Renee said, leaning back in her chair and feeling a snake pit of fury start to writhe in her stomach. "Don't you get it? Officially, I'm a single person in this company."

"That's *ridiculous*," Micki said. "It's rude. Clearly Owen has never done the guest list for a wedding before. You never invite anyone alone. Unless you're inviting a priest."

"Got weddings on the brain today, huh?" Renee felt her eyes sting for a second; she wished Micki would just clear out of her office now. It made her see red, the way some straight people, secure in their self-perception that they themselves were tolerant and accepting, were able to grossly underestimate the amount of discrimination that went on all around them. It was what made them cheerfully announce to friends of theirs, without permission, that you were gay, without stopping to consider for a second whether that person was a bigot, or might be in a position to do you harm.

"Hey, don't be upset. It's bound to be a head-to-toe bore. Better than a sedative. Celia would only hate it."

Renee gave her a tight smile. She did not feel like debating the fact that that was not the point.

"Tell you what," Micki said. "I won't bring John, either. You and I'll go together."

"Mick, that's really very . . . well-intentioned. But that's something you'd do for your dateless sorority sister. Don't you see there's a bigger issue here?"

"Well, of course I do." She took a few steps back, pulled at the top of her hair.

"Hey, I'm sorry. I don't mean to be a bitch. It

really is nice of you to offer. But it's not appropriate. Besides, I want to meet John." She smiled, genuinely this time.

"Okay." Micki hesitated. "Chill, though, all right?" She blew Renee a kiss and left.

"I think you should leave it alone," Celia said, pulling a thin pepperoni disk off her pizza slice and donating it to Renee.

"I can't. I can't even believe you're suggesting that." She was chewing her food without tasting it.

"You don't even get this worked up over your health insurance, which doesn't let you cover me," Celia said. "What's the big deal about one party?"

"Because the health insurance I know they're not going to go out on a limb about. They know they're in the majority and there's no reason to be a martyr over it. But this party — it's completely up to Owen. It's just hostile — husbands, wives and hetero live-ins only. Jesus, half the husbands in the office are screwing sources or the secretaries, anyway. And leaving an expense account trail, to boot. It's such bullshit."

"I think you're overreacting," Celia said. "I don't care if I don't go." She balled up her napkin and skidded it across the wood table.

"*I* care if you don't go. It should be our choice — not theirs. I worked as hard as anyone on this project. Harder."

"I know that. But you're talking to someone who still makes up stories about my dates with men for my manager, remember? Your boss knows your lover is a woman. I consider that something out of a science fiction movie."

"Exactly. They want points for tolerating you. They want congratulations for not firing you. But ultimately they want you to pass, to be like them, to be invisible. They want you to be grateful, not make waves, not ever make your life an *issue.*"

"You're right. That's what they want," Celia said, brushing a stray blonde curl out of the corner of her mouth. "And my parents want me to be cured in the morning, even though they love me – *and* you. And I can't make any of them not want those things. You wouldn't last a day at my company."

"You're right – I wouldn't."

"But I make more money at the hotehl than I ever dreamed I'd make, and I don't care if these people don't know a single lousy detail about my personal life," Celia said. "I don't even care if they know I'm feeding them a pack of lies. I don't need my job to be my family. I just need it to be my bread and butter."

They'd had this argument a hundred times and neither of them ever said anything different. It was the area they saw least eye-to-eye about and sometimes, in the middle of the argument, no matter how familiar their positions, Renee felt she was talking to a stranger. It didn't bother her just that Celia had a different view about such a key debate; it bothered her that they didn't agree.

"I still don't understand," Renee said. "You want me to tell my parents so badly."

"Because that's what family's about – love and acceptance. If it isn't, I don't know why people bother. It's crazy, these people who get together with their relatives just so they can all be rude and nasty to each other. But work is different. The hotel pays me to do a job. The rest is just not the point."

"Okay, so then Owen will have to tell me so. He'll have to draw the line in the sand."

Celia reached across the table and stroked Renee's knuckles. "Honey, I hate to see you so tortured all the time. Sometimes I wish you could take the world a little less *personally.*"

Renee, surveying her stockpile of pepperoni, refused to smile.

Owen was on the phone in his shirtsleeves, his feet up on his desk, pulling at his beard, when Renee finally got in to see him. Even after a year of his having come to *Pulse,* he still intimidated her. He had been hired away from the *Wall Street Journal* and since then had gotten nothing but good press about his changes at the magazine. The arrival of *Angle* was the first major threat to his reign; the whole office was dedicated to watching for any visible signs of strain in his manner. So far, no one had detected anything.

Renee wandered around his office, feigning interest in the same awards, plaques and framed photos she always looked at while he made her wait. She had never figured out if he expected her to comment on the phone conversations he conducted in her presence. If they'd truly been private, why would he gesture her in before he'd hung up?

"You tell the son of a bitch he can sue us as

soon as he feels like it. In fact, I look forward to further humiliating him in court, because we didn't even have the space to print all the shit we had on him." He frowned into the phone, his spiky silver eyebrows knitting together over the top of the receiver. "Yeah, I'll look over a memo, first, sure. Bye."

"Making friends in high places again, Owen?"

His moustache stretched upwards; that's how she could tell he was smiling. "What'cha got?"

"Look, about the party for the Companies Who Give Back. I seem to be the only one invited without a guest."

"Really? I thought I gave a husbands and wives okay to Phyllis." His brow wrinkled.

"Well, that would still leave me out, wouldn't it? Except that there's at least one living-together couple invited, and I *would* fall into that category. As you know."

"Sometimes Phyllis extrapolates a little bit. It's possible she just didn't know about your . . . situation."

"Yes, my situation." Renee had meant to stay professional; she instantly feared her words had sounded sneering.

"It's hard to keep up, Renee. Don't get sensitive on me." He drummed a pen on the edge of his desk.

"So I can bring my partner?"

He pulled at his beard.

"I've lived with her longer than some of these people have been married, Owen."

"I just don't want to make anyone uncomfortable,

Renee. I wouldn't want people to construe it as some kind of statement. It isn't the occasion for a statement. Of that kind."

Renee felt the room tilt slightly and silently cautioned herself to think before she spoke. "I don't plan to turn this into a coming-out party, if that's what you're worried about."

"It might create that kind of distraction, nonetheless." He was looking at her steadily.

"You're saying you really wish I wouldn't." She felt a slight tremble begin in her hands.

He smiled. "No. I'm saying I trust your judgment completely. That's one of your strengths. So I leave it up to you. You've heard my concerns."

"Yes. I have." She hoped she looked normal as she walked out of his office, because she felt stranger than she had in a long time.

"Honey, it amazes me every time. That you maintain enough optimism to still be disappointed." Celia massaged Renee's neck and shoulders in the dark.

Renee pulled up the covers and sighed loudly, but she couldn't make the feeling of pressure lift from her chest. All she knew was that keeping her body in contact with Celia's was somehow calming; she felt like a smashed glass that hadn't been glued together properly.

"You know what it is?" She rolled over and grabbed at Celia's hand. "It scares me. Because you never know exactly when they're going to turn on you. Or exactly what their limits are. You think, because you're having a normal conversation about it one minute, or because they know your *situation,* as he called it, that they're going the rest of the yardage with you. And then you slam right up against this brick wall. And they look at you like, Well, *of course* I meant it was okay for you to sleep in the barn, not in the big house with the other guests."

"That's right. And if you want to keep your life relatively ulcer-free, you say, Thank you for letting me sleep in your barn."

"*Goddamn* it, Celia."

"I know what you want, honey, and that you want it today. Or better yet, yesterday. But all these people will die eventually." She laughed at her own joke, looking as relaxed as a little girl at bedtime-story time.

"Now who's being optimistic?"

Celia wriggled closer; Renee could feel her breast nudging against her arm. "Look, there are just certain systems in place," Celia said. "Would you challenge a guy to a duel if he had a shotgun and you had a bow and arrow? Nothing will change at a company like yours or mine until there's somebody at Owen's level — or higher — who wants to take his or her lover to a function like this one. So why should you get yourself on his shit list? The only revenge is to do well. By their rules. Until you get to make your own."

"You know, if you were as hot-headed as me, just once, we could do some real damage."

"I struggle daily to resist your charms," Celia said against Renee's earlobe.

Renee put her arm around Celia's shoulders and felt her body slowly loosen into sleep. It was tempting, the idea of sleep, but she would resist. The least she could do was resist.

VISITATION

The road to Celia's parents' Florida house is flat and wide, smoothly paved, like an unlined face. It's a community of old people in a town in its infancy; just a year ago there was nothing here but lots with For Sale billboards pressed into swampy soil.

Celia has trouble thinking of her parents in a place like this, even to visit, let alone to live. Their house in Brooklyn had been more vertical than horizontal (every house in Florida seems to be a ranch) and it was nearly rancid with age the way loved old sneakers are. On weekends the house had always been loud and sweaty with relatives coming and going with their various miseries and triumphs — an auto shop that finally broke even, a cousin who needed an annulment quickly so he could marry an already-pregnant girlfriend. And everything had to be debated, and debated again, over an orgy of sticky, oozing, steaming food: lasagna and meatballs, breaded eggplant and parmigiana chicken, sfogliatellas and St. Joseph's cakes.

"It should be a right turn here," Renee says, hunched over a page of directions, her long brown hair falling forward and hiding her face. Celia recognizes the house from photos her mother has sent, a long, low, cream-colored house with two pink flamingo statues on the lawn. Everything is deep green and sunshine, and she has to remind herself that it's the middle of January.

"Hi girls! Hi!" her mother is shouting as she leans out the front door. "Bill, go help them with their bags," she yells over her shoulder.

Celia's father comes out to the car, grinning shyly. "You find it okay?" he says, wrapping them each in a hug. Both her parents treat Renee like another daughter. It's the best possible level of acceptance, she knows, but it makes her feel neuter. If they are both daughters, that makes them sisters. It takes her a few weeks to recharge sexually after they've spent time with her parents. But it's still better than being with Renee's parents — who don't know at all, or at least pretend not to, so that Celia spends her time with them getting knots in her gut, worried that she's going to slip and say something that will send the whole house of cards crashing down.

"The shrubs look great," Celia says, lingering in

front of the house, to her mother's great impatience. Her father is unofficially in charge of the outside of the house, her mother the inside. He has not yet gotten over the fact that he does not have to go to work every day. He still gets up the same time he always did when he had to drive to the post office, but Celia has not gotten him to say exactly what he does instead. Making coffee and reading the paper seem to have stretched into a three-hour ritual.

"Hi, hi, hi," her mother, wearing a flowered-print matching shorts-and-top set, says when they finally cross the threshold. She plants lipsticked kisses over both their faces as Celia's father grunts past with all the bags.

"Oh, the place looks beautiful, Catherine," Renee coos, and Celia's mother pulls herself into the posture of the lady of the house, gliding through the pink-and-cream rooms on the tour. Celia can imagine her wandering from room to room this way when she's by herself, just admiring and appraising. She is part of that generation of women for whom a nice house is more than just a material reward; it's an extension of personality.

She leads them out back and makes them sit on lounge chairs beside the pool, bringing them each an iced tea. "I sit out here in the morning with my coffee, before the sun gets to be too much," she says with a naughty smile, as if she has just confessed to some minor crime. And indeed, her mother's skin is a warm shade of milk chocolate, very hard for Celia to get used to after knowing her as a milky, urban white her whole life.

Her mother fills them in on the health of various family members, near and far, and the identities of couples new to the community. Already there are small cliques the newcomers must break into.

"Go on," Celia's father says, opening the sliding-glass doors, "put on your suits and take a swim. Your mother's chewing your ear off already." At sixty-five, he is still tall and broad-shouldered, and his hair seems not gray, just lighter, less intense.

Renee raises her eyebrows in interest and Celia encourages her, though she herself is content to recline and let the late afternoon sun turn her limbs to rubber. When Renee gets up and goes inside, Celia's father takes her seat.

"So how are you two? Okay?" he asks smiling, expecting, she sees, only good news. And that's all she delivers. She does not relay this summer's saga about Edie and Cole, and how it has shaken her to see them break up, seemingly without warning. From her parents' perspective, what her relationship with Renee lacks in conventionality, it makes up for in stability. She doesn't see any reason to deprive them of this comfort.

"A couple we know adopted a baby from Romania," Celia offers conversationally.

"Oh, really? From Romania?" her mother asks, as if this is the most unusual aspect of the arrangement.

"Yes. We went to the christening last month."

"The parish knew the situation?" her father asks. She can hear the caution in his voice; he is eager not to offend.

"One of them, Chrissie, stood up as the mother, and the other — as far as the church is concerned — is the godmother. The parish didn't seem to have any problem with a single woman adopting an orphan." Celia considers it a rotten deal to strike. She would

not want to be in Eileen's shoes, having to pretend —
even for an hour — to be a concerned friend rather
than the other mother. But then, she wouldn't have
lied at all to win the approval of a church that
would only condemn her if it knew the truth.

"Neither one of them wanted to get pregnant?"
her mother asks. "I thought that's what lesbian
couples did — got inseminated. I saw it on *Sally
Jessy.*"

It's still a shock to Celia to hear the word
"lesbian" cross her mother's lips so casually; she has
to remember to give her credit for keeping up. "Well,
some do. But neither of these women wanted to go
through that right now at work. Eileen's a lawyer and
Chrissie's an accountant, and they're both at pretty
conservative firms. Besides, I think Chrissie is really
the one who wanted a baby and Eileen is kind of
going along. It's one of the things that made Chrissie
stay in her marriage longer than she wanted to. She
hated the idea of not being able to have kids." She
pauses to let this sink in. "So she might get pregnant
later. But right now they figured they'd give a kid a
home who needed it."

Renee re-emerges, wearing a bathing suit Celia has
not seen on her yet. It's black with a hot pink V
slicing down the torso, the point ending just above
her crotch. She walks by, fussing with her ponytail,
smiling at them politely as if they are strangers at a
hotel pool. Celia guesses that Renee senses she has
walked back in on a charged conversation and
doesn't want to be disruptive. She dives into the
water almost noiselessly.

Celia sees her mother's eyelids start to wilt with

the heat and the excitement and probably the time of day — this long midsection of afternoon that animals and cultures not yet completely divorced from their natural rhythms still sacrifice to sleep. Celia and her father resist, watching Renee swim the length of the pool, sometimes on her back, sometimes on her side.

"You two never think about having kids?" he asks.

Celia stiffens; as an only child, she knows that the announcement of her lesbianism eight years ago carried with it at least a double devastation: no marriage, no grandchildren. "No, I don't think so, Dad. Not right now, anyway. But there's no telling if we'll change our minds. After all, we're young yet." She notes the irony; it was as a child that she learned from her father this tactic of holding out hope, no matter how remote: a grandfather who might not die after all, the dog they might someday have.

He nods; they watch the surface of the pool crease and fold, dark and light, like suede, as Renee swims. "Would be funny," he says, smiling. "Be almost like a real family."

That night they go out to dinner, ignoring weather reports of an impending thunderstorm. They eat at a Chinese restaurant that Celia's parents have deemed "not bad." The only disappointment of their southern migration is the poor quality of ethnic food. Especially the Italian, which has been a nearly uniform and unspeakable affront to them.

When they return home and pull into the

driveway, Celia nudges Renee, pointing out the dozens of cars parked in front of the house next door. "Hey, your neighbors like to throw wild parties?" Renee asks.

"Oh, them?" Celia's mother answers. Tonight she is wearing a turquoise jumpsuit and matching pumps. Celia doesn't remember her mother going in for so much color back in Brooklyn. "Not parties, not exactly."

Celia frowns across the way at the house. It's true, it seems too quiet and dark to justify anything festive. "What, then?"

"Well, it seems to be a religious vigil, actually," she goes on.

"What does that mean? What kind of vigil?"

"This couple," her father says, "claim the Virgin Mary appears to them. Next thing you know, word starts to get around, and people start showing up here on Sundays, hoping to catch the next visitation."

Celia waits, expecting her parents to make some appropriately mocking remark, but they don't. There is nothing inspired about her parents' faith; it was learned and is now automatic, like manners. It does not have any of the fever pitch of passion, or the flamboyance of hysteria. Not for them weeping statues, faces in cloth, apparitions on the hillside. "You don't believe them, do you?" Celia asks.

"No, but you don't have to sound so appalled. They're all very nice people," her mother says, getting out and closing the car door soundly. "It's not like it's one of these healing groups, where they chant and sing in the backyard or claim snakes turn into sticks. Or vice versa, whatever they do. Basically they just sit quietly and wait. Till dawn."

Celia catches Renee's eye and is relieved to see she also seems alarmed. "You're not involved with them, are you?"

"Oh, no," Celia's mother says quickly. She puts up a kettle of hot water for late-night coffee. "We just worry about, you know, the neighborhood. Tell them, Bill. He knows more about the ins and outs."

"There's another couple here from Pennsylvania who are very upset. *Very* upset," her father says. "They say they've seen this kind of thing get out of control. You get thousands of people coming from all over the country. People selling key chains and renting out their homes like bed-and-breakfast inns. Port-a-Sans along the roadside. Church officials have to come in and verify the authenticity. Next thing you know, your neighborhood's not your own. It's like living at the county fair all year round."

"So what's this Pennsylvania couple planning to do about it?" Celia has fallen into her parents' habit of identifying people by the state they're originally from.

"Well, they tried to start a petition, bring it to the mayor," her father says. "But you know, there's no law against having people over to your house, no matter how many. And they don't make any noise late at night, or sell things, or park illegally. Not yet, anyway."

Renee is looking out the sliding glass door into

the next yard. Celia joins her, and sees scores of them sitting on the lawn like some geriatric Woodstock. They're as still as cats stalking birds.

"Why would anybody believe the Virgin Mary would appear to this couple as opposed to anybody else?" Renee asks.

"I don't know, really," Celia's father answers. "But you have to admit, not that many other people make the claim, so it's not like they've got a lot of competition." He smiles at his own mild joke. "The husband had a heart attack last year and no one expected him to live. And when he pulled through, he started telling people the Blessed Virgin appeared to him and told him he had a special mission to help bring people back to the Church."

"Gee, seems like a long shot," Celia says. "Why didn't she just tell him to have the Pope strike the celibacy rule for priests?"

"Shhh," her mother says. "Don't make fun. You don't know if your voice carries. Nothing's too well insulated down here."

Her mother has made up the guest room for them, laying out plush blue towels with white satin sea shells embroidered at the bottom. Celia and Renee get into bed, unused to wearing pajamas. At home they sleep nude, liking the random brush of their bare buttocks against each other, or, before falling asleep, the chance to drowsily mouth a nipple or trace patterns with slow fingers in the warmth between the other's legs.

But tonight, pajama-clad, they argue again about

Renee's not yet having told her own parents about them. Renee, as usual, maintains that there's no reason to force unhappy news on them, and Celia still can't make her see why the silence and subterfuge bother her, still cannot convince her that she is not giving her parents enough credit for having grown up a little, too.

Once Renee is asleep, very little except an alarm clock, will wake her. When they're home, if Celia cant's sleep, she'll sometimes get up for an hour or two to read in the living room, and Renee will have had no idea. Celia teases her that if she ever wanted to have an affair, she'd know exactly when she could get away with it.

So it's not unusual that the noise did not rouse Renee but has left Celia staring, sweaty with indecision, at the ceiling. It sounded to her like the woosh of the sliding glass door. She knows it can't be an intruder, not without triggering the alarm system — a lifestyle tic that most of the Northeasterners carried down with them.

She gets up and looks out the window of their room, which faces the backyard. The night here, without the artificial light of store signs and traffic, is dense. It's like trying to make out something clearly in a photographic negative — everything is just one shade of dark upon another. She manages to make out a tall figure working its way slowly toward the yard next door, where people are still sitting, frozen in place, like lawn ornaments. The figure's clothes flap and flutter at the arms and legs like a flag in the wind.

Curiosity overtakes fear, and Celia throws on a robe and goes down to the living room. The sliding glass door is unlocked. She pulls it open holding her breath, but is met with only the clicking of crickets. She closes it behind her and heads barefoot across the wet, spiky grass.

The yard people are as quiet as they look from a distance, but Celia senses a kind of collective breathing from them. It's as if the lawn is alive with concentration. She pulls the robe more tightly around herself; the night air is damp and desert-cool.

One figure is sitting along the periphery, apart from the tight cluster that makes the large center, and Celia heads toward it, unafraid. Many of the people, she can see now, are sitting with their heads bowed forward, but whether they're sleeping or praying she can't say. This figure is alert, forward-facing, watchful. She has to get within two feet before she's sure who it is.

"Dad," she whispers, squatting, a hand on his pajama-clad arm.

He shudders, then looks up and smiles sadly. He puts a finger to his lips to silence her. Then he pats a space next to him on what seems to be a canvas mat.

Slowly the blackness lightens into shadows; she can see the forest of torsos sitting across the entire yard. From a distance they were silent; now she hears them, the rustle of their clothes as they shift, the creak of joints, the inhale and exhale of breath, even the sound of their watching, of eyes moving along the horizon, like a finger across a page.

It's the closest she comes to being in church again, something she hasn't done since high school, with the exception of her grandmother's funeral. The silence was the one thing she missed, the intimate silence of a crowd of strangers who had agreed, for the hour, at least, to cast their lot as one.

And it's easy in the dark, so close to her father that she can feel the field of heat around him, to fall into communion with this group, faceless though it is. Plenty of people — and she is often among them, she admits — find it easy to poke fun at those who make no secret of believiing that there's some higher power, or even just some organizing principle, to the universe they all live in. But wasn't it just as daft, preposterous, reckless, to believe that there was none at all?

Her father gets to his feet and gestures for her to follow him back across the yard to their own house. The mud sucks sensuously at her arches, the grass pokes sharply, coldly, between her toes.

They sit down in the lawn chairs next to the pool, the water now silvery-black like pewter. They'll have to wipe their feet before they go back in or her mother will be suicidal with despair over the wrecked rug. Celia prefers to focus on this smaller, domestic dilemma than on the larger one of her father's behavior. She waits for him to explain.

"I've gone over there a few times," he begins, whispering. "I was curious — all those people." He shrugs. "I didn't tell your mother, didn't want to worry her, have her thinking I had loose marbles." He looks at Celia now, making the silent request.

Celia nods, though she is unused to having a secret with one parent and not the other.

"It's kind of peaceful. I started to like it. You're with all these people, but you don't have to know them well, don't have to small-talk, don't have to discover all the things about them that make them mean or annoying. You can just sort of think, you know, *humanity.*" He cups his hands into the shape of a globe.

"They're all out here because they want something," he goes on. "Some of them are sick, or love someone who's sick. Some of them can't bear to think this is all there is — work for forty years and retire to wait to die. Some of them feel they need to be forgiven for something."

Celia doesn't ask how he knows all this; she doesn't want to interrupt.

"I guess I wanted something, too. I was worried about you."

Celia literally jumps; she is not prepared. It was easy to imagine him in one of the other categories he mentioned. "Me?" she rasps. "You went because of *me?*"

"The way I was raised, you know, the way you're living is a sin."

Celia feels as if she's been speared to the chair.

"I love you, honey, you know that." He reaches over and squeezes her arm. "And if I was in charge, nothing bad would ever happen to you. But, you know, the church teaches, the church teaches that . . ." He looks away and she sees his shoulders shaking.

Her body is on fire with panic, and yet all she's able to do is sit there, still as one of the lawn people. A good five minutes pass in silence and she knows her father is wrestling with images of Hell.

"I thought what I'd do, you know, if she came," he says finally, "was ask her to make an exception."

"Daddy." Celia gets up now, stands behind his chair and puts her arms around his shoulders. She thinks to say: Jesus protected a prostitute. Jesus loved a man he knew would betray him. Jesus forgave another who denied him to save his own neck. She knows that using the stories he believes in would comfort him, give him hope. But as much as she wants to ease his private torment, she can't bring herself to compare herself and Renee to whores, turncoats and cowards. She realizes what she wants more than his peace of mind is for him to denounce a whole lifetime of belief because it hasn't made room for a person like herself.

The night is full of shadows; it would be possible to think you saw just about anything out here now. She focuses on getting them both back into the house and into bed, but there is still the problem of their muddy feet.

She looks around and sees a watering can at the corner of the patio. She dips it into the dark water of the pool and carries it back to where her father is sitting. Crouching, she pours it over his feet, and they giggle a little with the shock of its coldness. The towel Renee had used this afternoon is still tossed across another chair; Celia uses it to pat her father's feet dry.

She starts to head back to the pool with the can, but he tells her to sit and takes the can from her. He repeats the ritual, watering her feet with the deliberateness of the gardener he has recently become. He dries her feet and then pulls open the sliding glass door for them.

Just then, a streak of light breaks open the sky and disappears again. The lawn people stand, as if on cue, and release a collective *Ooooh.*

Her father smiles a melancholy smile, then shrugs. Celia would laugh if she weren't so close to tears. Neither of them says what they believe.

QUEER FATE

"*Did you do it, you sonofabitch?*" she screams into the phone before I even get it all the way up to my ear. She's crying so hard I can barely understand her.

"Do what? Do *what?*"

"YOU LYING SONOFABITCH, YOU KNOW WHAT."

"Chrissie, I don't," I say. I'm scared by now.

"Eileen and I have seen you plenty of times — *plenty* of times — cruising by here, just looking. I don't know what you think you're going to see. How could you *do* it, Mike?"

"Do what?" She has *me* screaming now.

"You're pathetic," she says before slamming down the phone.

When people ask me, I tell them the truth. Yeah, I say, my wife left me. She left me for a woman. It's a queer fate, I say — get it?

Then they want to know: Did I see it coming? How are you supposed to see a thing like that coming? I mean, I *married* her. She was somebody's wife. She was *my* wife, for God's sake.

How I met her, they want to know next. The usual way. It wasn't like I took out an ad, asking for a girl with latent lesbian tendencies. We used to go to the same deli at lunchtime almost every day. She got only one of two things: liverwurst on rye or egg salad on white toast. And I got whatever the special was. Whatever it was. The deli guys used to flirt with her — she was a standout, that's the truth. So much for thinking you can tell just by looking. I'd like to tell them: Remember Chrissie? Goddamn latent lesbian. And I *married* her, for God's sake.

We were married for three years, and I never saw it coming. I gave it to her pretty good, she used to say so. She used to moan for me, I could make her moan. She liked to get laid as much as I did, maybe more. I mean, that's just my opinion, but what the hell do I know about it, right? A guy whose wife leaves him for another woman.

Thing is, this other one, the dyke, the one who

102

must have converted her, was a pretty good view herself. The Dyke Who Came To Dinner, I called her. Later, I mean. Because at first, they were just best girlfriends. At least, that's what I thought. But after a while I figured it out. I mean, a thirty-year-old wife doesn't have sleepovers with a girlfriend. There was no reason for her not to come home to her husband, especially when the dyke lived just across town, we're talking all of twenty minutes away. At first I thought it was a kinky thing, you know, she'd expect me to join them. I was into that okay. But it wasn't like that. It was like she found religion or something. Another goddamn woman. I never saw it coming and no, I absolutely do *not* blame myself.

Thing is, I love Chrissie. Jesus, I love her. Everything else is — you know, it just isn't Chrissie.

I kept wracking my brain: Where'd she meet the dyke? I guess they have bars, right? She must have been going to bars, right? Jesus, Chrissie in a dyke bar. I tell you, it makes me want to puke. And she was *married*. To me, for God's sake.

I said, Chrissie, did you ever do this kind of thing before? Before I *married* you, for God's sake? The next thing I know, she's telling me she's into women, all the way, all the time, and she thought maybe she always had been. So like, why the hell am I hearing about it only now, three years and one set of marriage vows later? She still loved me, she said. But she was *in* love with the dyke. This dyke who ate dinner in my house, at my dinner table, and Jesus Christ, when my back is turned, she's eating my wife.

That's the kind of thing that would make her scream till I thought her lungs would rattle. "DON'T

USE THAT LANGUAGE!" she'd say, like she had some goddamn right to be righteous when here she is, *my wife,* having an extra-marital affair, and not even a normal one at that. Instead this sick thing that really, when I think about it, makes me want to puke. Where do you think it comes from, anyway? Jesus, it's so sick. Am I wrong? And you can't tell by looking, boy, that's bullshit, let me tell you.

So Chrissie moved across town, into the dyke's house. I don't get it, myself, why she wanted to trade. I don't see it. You're going along in your life, doing everything right. Got a good job. Got a husband who loves you. Going to have a family soon. And then you go and deliberately live like a pervert. It's as though she got this illness, like a cancer. I know some people these days are too polite to say that out loud. But I can say it, I *married* her, for God's sake.

Try to understand, Mike, she'd say. It's just my stripes, I can't help it. Nothing personal, really. *Right.* She just met the dyke, she said, and all the feelings she'd been beating back just rushed forward and there she was, in love, whether she liked it or not. All I know is, I told her, if I got the urge, say, to root around in some school kid's underwear, I'd control myself, for God's sake. And I certainly wouldn't wreck my whole life over it. A married woman, for God's sake, it's a disgrace. "DON'T COMPARE ME TO A PEDOPHILE," she'd scream, peeling the paint, rattling her lungs. "YOU'RE SO DENSE," she'd tell me. *I'm* dense, that's a laugh. Excuse me, but the last time I checked, people who got married maybe couldn't be expected to have picked the right *individual*, but generally they could be counted on to have picked the right sex.

Anyway, she moved in with the dyke. I drive by there some nights, sometimes I have to get loaded first. I know where they live. But I never see them. They're always out. Or in. Eating. I was her *husband*. I have rights. I deserve some explanation.

My friend Pete says I'm crazy to put up with it. You just grab the bitch by the hair and take her home. Can't you get arrested for sodomy in this state? Tell her it's your house or county jail, take her pick. The cops'll even let you haul off and clip her one, too — they don't like to get mixed up with that domestic violence shit. But start talking about disturbing public morals, or whatever it's called, and they're interested.

But you know, I don't want Chrissie back that way. I want her to want me like she used to, all on her own.

I go directly to the house where Chrissie is living, and I see it right away. Goose bumps crawl across my scalp, that's how scared I get, seeing it like that in broad daylight. And a voice in me says: *Good*. Good, they deserve it. Maybe this will do it — scare her back to her senses, back to me. That's all I really want, I don't wish her any harm.

I look up just as she's coming through the diner

door, rattling the little tin bell as she pushes the door open. She sees me right away and heads over, her face a fist, rage and blame all squeezed on to it so plainly I wonder why she agreed to meet me at all.

"Hey," I say as she slips into the seat across from me. I deliberately got us a booth in the back.

She meets my eyes for a second, scornfully, then scans the menu. We ate here so many times when we were still living together that I know she has it memorized. The only thing that's ever changed are the prices; there's scrawl over some of the lower numbers in reedy ballpoint writing.

She closes the menu. "You're here to tell me to my face you didn't do it."

"That's right." I jump a little, not because she sounds so mean, but because when her eyes are on me, when she's talking to me so close, my breath still catches a little below my ribs. Her blue eyes are the same but her hair is shorn like a lamb, the dark waves smoothed close to the side of her head. The top is a little longer and tufted.

"God, you are still easy on the eyes, babe." I reach across the table for her hand, a second after my brain tells me what a stupid mistake it is.

"Don't, Mike. I told you a thousand times, I don't need saving."

I lean against my seat and hear the booth hiss a little with the pressure of my back. A waitress brings us coffee and takes our order.

"Eileen and I are thinking of just leaving the house the way it is."

"That's about the stupidest goddamn thing I ever heard," I say.

"It's called making a point."

"It's called being a hump."

"None of this would've happened, Mike, if you weren't such an asshole. I had no idea, I had absolutely no idea, that you were capable of something like this. You weren't the only one who got some surprises in our marriage. I thought better of you, all along."

She was my *wife,* up to only a few months ago. I try to hate her now, but all I feel is that I want to cry. "Look, this much is true. I did used to drive by your house some nights. I was looking for you. I never saw you once, though. I thought I had a right. But I didn't do that to the house."

The waitress puts our soup and sandwiches down and Chrissie spends a long time inspecting everything, stirring and cutting and rearranging. I watch her long fingers. There's a ring I don't recognizie.

"I want to believe you, Mike. I really do."

My cheeks go hot and I hear Pete again, saying I'm crazy to put up with it. *You just grab the bitch by the hair.* "If I ever find out who did it, Chrissie, I'll make him pay for it, I swear to God, I —"

"If it wasn't you, Mike, I really don't care."

I stop chewing.

"I don't care about the random crazies. What can I do if some stranger who doesn't know a thing about me hates my guts? But if it's someone you love, well — that's close to home. Then you've got a fight on your hands."

I try to think what she wants me to feel. "It's just not natural, Chrissie," I say finally.

"Well, maybe not. But it's true."

* * * * *

I get to the bar before it's full and just like I thought, Pete is there already, stationed on a stool, a sentry in the soggy air.

"Buddy," he says, an arm out, aiming for my back. "How are ya?"

I sit down, leaving a stool between us. "I've been better." The bartender brings me a mug of beer. The handle's so icy cold my fingers stick to it for a second.

"We've got to get you back in circulation. Too many dates with dirty videos, and not enough with a real woman. Hey, maybe Chrissie'll show up in one of them, you know, in a shot where they put two women in a room with a bowl of dildos —"

"Knock it off — she's still my wife, you prick," I say, the neck of his T-shirt suddenly bunched in my fist. I'm picking him up a little off his stool, I can feel it.

"Lay off," he says, slow and monotone as his hand closes tight around my wrist. We let go at the same time.

I consider apologizing: Pete's as crazy as they come. I know some of the stuff he's done to people just for the kicks of it. I know he was doing me a favor making me back down just now. I take a long swig of the beer.

"That's right, have a drink, buddy. No hard feelings. I know she's got you running ragged." He pats me on the back.

"I don't know what to do anymore."

"It's simple. You gotta do something to get her back. You're not gonna rest until you get her back."

He's right. That's the goddamnedest thing about Pete. He's right about a lot of things.

* * * * *

I'm waiting outside Eileen's office when she gets off work. She starts to head right past the car, but I honk, and she stops in her tracks.

"Eileen," I call out the window. "Can I talk to you? It's me, Mike. Just for a little while?"

She approaches the car warily and stops too far away to have a normal conversation. I have to keep shouting.

"Come on, just get in for a minute. I need to talk to you." I lean across the seat and shove the passenger door open. My heart speeds up a little bit. Truth is, I have no idea what I'm going to say to her.

She puts her hand on the door, and looks up and down the block, considering. I'd never have picked her for a dyke, that's for sure. She's got shoulder-length blonde hair and a good body. Dresses sharp, too. She settles onto the seat next to me and folds her arms. She still hasn't said a word.

"You gonna close the door?" I say.

"I don't see why. Are we going someplace?"

"I'll drive you home."

She laughs, but it's got a sour ring to it. "Drive me home, that's a good one."

"I didn't do that to the house, Eileen. It's like I told Chrissie." I'm gripping the wheel with both hands.

"Why don't you just leave us alone?" She starts to get out.

"Stay in the car, Eileen," I say, and now I'm sorry I don't have anything to make her stay. Pete said I should have something to make her stay and listen, take me seriously, but I'm not Pete. I can't do it Pete's way.

"Are you threatening me?" She's glaring.

"No, I'm begging you. Just let me drive you home. Please."

She slams the car door shut like a threat of her own and keeps looking at me, like I'm a wild animal on the wrong side of the cage.

I pull the car away from the curb easy. We've got only about a ten-minute drive so I don't have much time. "How's business? Winning all your cases?"

"Enough."

We drive a few blocks in silence. "Look, you obviously don't feel like chatting, so let me say what I gotta say. That day I saw Chrissie — we didn't just talk. She came home with me, we went to bed, she told me she wants to come back. But she can't bring herself to tell you —"

"My God, you're *pathe*tic."

"I know it's hard for you to believe, Eileen. But believe me, most people would say it's harder to believe she left me for a woman. So it's not so odd at all that she would go back to a man, to her husband."

"Stop this goddamn car." Her voice is like something on ice and she's got both hands on the door, her eyes on the road, waiting for her chance. Something snaps; I floor the gas.

"Stay in the fucking car and *listen* to me, Eileen." I'm flying by everyone on the road. I take a right down a side street so I don't have to get stopped by lights, or be forced to run them. "Listen to me, bitch. She came to the house and we screwed our brains out and she barely remembered your name by the end of it. She thinks *you're* pathetic." I have to swerve so I didn't rear-end a car that's suddenly in front of us. "A woman who's got to go around stealing other people's wives."

"Let me out of this car or so help me, God . . ."

"Go ahead, get out," I say. I lick the sweat off my upper lip and pump the car up a notch faster. "Go ahead, go ahead!"

"You're going to kill us both," she says. I hear it now: Fear. Real fear. I slam on the brakes. She rocks forward.

"Sorry I took you out of your way." I lean back into the seat. "When you get home, give Chrissie my love." And I wink.

Not a lot of people would blame me, not most people, even. She was my wife. That means something to most people. It means you've got certain rights, rights to fight back, too. She used to love me, she used to say I had kind eyes.

When I start down the block, it hits me again as hard as the first time. You can't miss it, really, not even a block away. Hot pink words, screaming filthy accusations all over it, clear across the windows, dripping down the front steps. The letters fizz away at the ends, like hot pink soda bubbles. It makes me feel like I have tracks through my gut and a train just came screeching through, that's how scared I get every time I see it.

"Holy shit," Pete whispers. "Holy shit. They've been living in it like that?"

We had to drive back and forth to the hardware

store a few times before we got the exact right shade of white. You'd think white is white, but it's not in the paint world, where you can have China white or Aztec white or Atrium white or, or, or. It takes two full weeks' salary for me to buy enough for the whole house, and the trays and the rollers. Luckily I have my own ladder, and Pete is going to help me. We figure we can have the house done before either of them gets home from work.

Pete gets out of the car ahead of me, the ladder across his shoulder like a rifle. I go around to the trunk to unload the cans. I lift them out, one by one, and line them up on the curb. Her lawn could use a seeding, I think, and more watering. Does she think of me at all, I wonder, and how I used to break my back getting our lawn all thick and plush like a golf course? Does she still like to make love in the daylight? Does she still use a baby voice when she's trying to get her way?

I try to think what I'll say to Chrissie when she calls to ask about the house being painted over. I practice: I didn't do it to the house the first time, it wasn't me. It could have been anyone. It could have been one of your neighbors, even — people have eyes. Maybe someone doesn't want a pair like you down the block. It happens all the time. I know everything points to it being me, everyone thinks so, even Pete. But it wasn't. I didn't do it. Except I guess it doesn't matter because, you know, I might as well have.

I guess I might as well have.

SISTER

This is what I know about the woman who loved my mother: She was my mother's cousin and best friend, and as soon as she was able to, she became a nun.

She entered the convent in 1950.

I don't remember meeting her even though there are pictures to prove that I did. I'm about three in these, old enough to hold onto some shred of memory, but I recall nothing. Sometimes I wonder if I ran across the right kind of heavy cotton, stiff with starch, stale with too little sunshine and fresh air, whether I might unleash some buried impression of her and know what it felt like to stand next to her as she towered above me in her massive shoes and layers of scratchy, black cloth, her huge, scary habit making her face look beaky and birdlike. And I would like to know, because, since she loved my mother, I wonder what she made of me.

By the time I was in high school, very few of the nuns wore any kind of special clothing. Apart from a modest gratuitous habit and Red Cross pumps, they looked like anyone else. They did not wear the shroud, the shackles, the forbidding armor, of the woman who loved my mother.

She did not write to anyone from the convent except her own mother, and my mother. There were no old boyfriends for her to mourn.

It was a noble thing in 1950 to be a nun. She had the calling, my mother says.

It's perhaps perverse to wish, in retrospect, that my mother's cousin had had the courage for her real calling, because, who knows, then I might never have been born at all. But I wish for it anyway. I wish she had not wasted her life, gone unloved, been locked away, never known passion, had only to write letters to a married woman who did not love her back the same way.

"*Dearest Angela,*" the letters all began. "*How wonderful that God has blessed you with a beautiful, healthy daughter. I've prayed for it, and God has answered my prayers. It was wonderful to see you all on Sunday. You are the kind of family the Church rejoices over. May God bless your little Renee.*"

She never mentioned my father by name.

She never said: You are the kind of family that sent me into exile.

I'm sure she must have inspired swooning in a few young girls. She, with her strong hands and serious face, her body a tall, straight-lined mystery under the curtains of black robes. Because to lust after a nun it is not necessary to think about a body: it is only necessary to think about the soul. That's why so many young girls swoon.

There would have been one young girl, a lover of poetry, who sat in the front row always, who raised her hand often, who stayed behind, who helped on weekends. One young girl who would have had her mother worried, her boyfriends frustrated. One young girl whom my mother's cousin would never have written about, would barely have let herself think about. One young girl who, when the nun didn't return one Monday, would have felt such a fissure of grief that she would never come back together again the same way.

What my mother wrote back she's not exactly sure. But the letters all began: *Dear Sister.* No longer could she use the name she had whispered across a

115

pillow during sleepovers, no longer could she giggle about the attentions of a young Marine, wonder about the secret rituals of married life.

In one picture my mother's cousin is standing in our backyard; behind her is a white picket fence and I am pressed against her robes, awkwardly, as if the person taking the picture had shoved me there against my will. She is grinning hard, almost hard enough, it seems, to push the habit and wimple off her head. She looks about as natural with me at her side as a Cadillac in a swimming pool. I look as if I am about to cry.

That one young girl, that lover of poetry, was me ten years later with another nun. The day of my graduation from grammar school, there was chaotic celebration in the classroom but I was mournful and uneasy. This nun was not tall and strong; she was petite and pretty, and my devotion to her had made my mother jealous and broody. She was moving through the group of us eighth graders, giving her best wishes, and I felt her aiming her journey at me where I stood with a small circle of popular girls who were soon to be out of my orbit, swept away by their fascination with high school boys. Then she was in front of me, saying things about what a pleasure it had been to have me in her class, how she expected great things of me in the future, and then I was up on my toes, reckless with desperation, pressing my lips to her cheek, and fleeing. Fleeing because I knew that what I felt was hopeless, forbidden, and maybe even fatal.

* * * * *

"*Dearest Angela,*" another letter on ruled white paper began. "*My mother wrote to tell me you went to visit her with little Renee, and she told me how beautiful and friendly she is. I can hardly wait to see her again. Motherhood is a calling, too, Angela, and children are truly one of His most miraculous joys. I pray for you all often.*"

My mother takes these out sometimes and reads them, as if they have just arrived anew, as if she is still just thinking of how to answer, of what to say to a woman she still loves, but with whom she has less and less in common.

Another five years later it was me with another woman, this one planning to become a nun. When we met, the summer would be over in just a few weeks and her destination was the convent and mine was college. We had met in a straight bar, she with her friends, I with mine. Somebody who was giving her a ride ended up meeting a guy, and I ended up driving her home, and then she ended up with her hand under my T-shirt, under my bra, her fingers scissoring over my nipple like she knew what she was doing, knew what she was after . . . sister, sister, *sister.*

We met every night for the next three weeks. She lasted a week at the convent and then joined me in Massachusetts. We were crazy hot lovers for a year. And when it was over, I almost had to remember to be sad. Because I was just so gleeful. You didn't get that one, I said, every time I passed a church. An eye for an eye. Hallelujah.

In the convent in the 1950s, nuns offered up their suffering to God. They reeled around with migraines, hacked their way through bronchitis, hobbled and limped on sprains and ripped tendons. Because to ask for comfort for the body was seen as a weakness of the spirit.

The death certificate for the woman who loved my mother said brain hemorrhage. There was no warning and little pain and of course it is the truth. Because the Church has never lied. Because everyone is happy there. And everyone is free to go.

BABY TALK

The baby was as dense and compact as a bag of wet cement; Renee was surprised by the little body's concentrated weight. It lay across her lap with the still seriousness of a miniature Buddha, a warm, sweet smell rising up off the top of its downy head.

"Want me to take her for a while?" Chrissie asked, smiling, already working her hands under the baby's armpits. Chrissie's rescue was well-intentioned – Renee was sure her own nervous uncertainty was apparent – but it was also self-serving. Chrissie's hunger for the baby was ferocious. Renee thought that if she were Eileen, she would be a little jealous.

"Who's my Annie-pie sweetcake?" Chrissie singsonged at the baby as she jostled her gently over her head. The baby broke into a heart-shaped smile as a reward, her cheeks bunching into balls.

"See that?" said Eileen, at the stove, stirring sauce as she watched Annie dangling over Chrissie's head. "We start out in life fearless. Babies would probably be champion bungee-jumpers. It's only later that we learn to become wimps."

"Makes sense to me," Celia said. She took another piece of brie on a cracker from the tray on the kitchen table. "The older you get, the more you realize how much you have to lose."

"What do you think, honey?" Eileen asked. "Will she let you put her down? The food's almost ready."

"Yes, she's ready, aren't you, dumpling? Beddy-bye time?" Chrissie said to the baby, rubbing noses with her and winning another blissed-out smile. "She's such a good little girl," Chrissie said to them all before she disappeared into the next room.

Renee caught Celia's eye. They had debated this the whole car ride into south Jersey: Had Eileen even wanted a baby at all? Or did she agree to it because she was afraid to risk Chrissie's discontent? There were things, Renee imagined, that haunted you when you took up with a woman whose last lover was her husband.

"I'm really glad you guys could make it out to see us," Eileen said, carrying the wine glasses into the dining room. "You usually can't catch a New Yorker out here with a search squad." Renee followed her in, marveling at the fact of the dining room, not to

120

mention the sheer size of it. By comparison, hers and Celia's apartment seemed dorm-like.

"It's because we live in Brooklyn," Celia said. "Since we don't live in Manhattan, we already know what it's like to be social outcasts."

"And we also didn't mind that BYOB means Bring Your Own Bib," Renee teased.

"Oh, speaking of which, I can't believe I forgot to tell you," Eileen said. "The nanny quit. On the way out yesterday, she said she wouldn't be coming back anymore. Just like that."

"You're kidding? How rotten. Now what are you going to do?" Celia asked.

"But wait a minute," Renee interrupted. "Didn't she even say why?"

Eileen sat at the edge of one of the beige lacquered dining room table chairs. "Of course I got paranoid. But she knew about us from the beginning — I told you that, right? We wouldn't have had it any other way. But I think it just got to her after a month or so. I don't know what exactly wigged her out, but she slunk out of here like she was shedding her criminal past or something. Guilt by association. I think in her chats with her nanny friends, she felt like there was something wrong with her for liking us, for not minding working for us."

"God, I hope you're wrong," Renee said. "I'd much rather think she decided you were a hysterical tyrant."

"No, she knew that from the beginning, too."

"Knew what?" Chrissie said as she came back into the room and put her arms around Eileen's shoulders.

"We just heard about the runaway nanny," Celia said.

"Yeah. I'm taking this week off — which I was saving for vacation — to do an emergency search for another one. The agency owes us more candidates by contract, since the first one walked after only a month."

Eileen urged them all to take a seat as she got up and brought a huge wooden bowl of tossed salad, colorful with peppers, cucumbers, radishes and tomatoes, and served their portions of ziti and chicken cordon bleu. Eileen was the cook of the pair; Renee had watched her sauté eggplant or mix a dip with the same intensity that she argued a case in court.

"Did she go right out, honey?" Eileen asked Chrissie.

"Like a light."

"She's a lucky little girl," Celia said, rummaging through the salad to pile her plate with pepper slices and tomato. "To be so loved."

"We're luckier — to have her," Chrissie said. "You know, when we were in Romania, I felt a little bit like the marauding Americans, buying up foreigners' babies because their governments had made them so poor they couldn't afford to raise their own children." She cast her blue eyes down for a moment, her face clouded, and fiddled with her utensils. "The head nurse at the orphanage — she was really cool. I tried to tell her I felt like we were kidnapping these babies from their own heritage. She just shook her head and said, 'You see this little baby? Do you think she owes more to the soil than to her soul?'" Chrissie smiled, her eyes shiny with tears. Eileen draped an arm around her narrow shoulders and squeezed.

After dessert, Eileen and Chrissie narrated the video of their trip to Romania; Renee kept waiting for some glimpse of the country, of city streets, but all they got were shots inside orphanages and motel rooms, close-ups of little Annie, sleeping, smiling, spitting up.

"It must be hard to believe she's really here — you were planning to adopt all the way back when we first met you."

They had met Eileen and Chrissie two years ago, on an all-lesbian cruise to Mexico. Renee remembered that they had noticed Chrissie first, not just because she was so good-looking with her coffee-colored hair and neat, sharp features, but because she had a kind of glossy straight-girl aura that made them wonder if she had wandered onto the wrong boat. When Eileen showed up with her at dinner, acting the solicitous part of the smitten honeymooner, they were relieved for more reasons than one.

They watched more shots of Annie crawling, Annie crying, Annie chewing. Chrissie seemed to figure largely in nearly every frame. "So has everyone been obnoxiously treating you like the Daddy, now, Eileen?" Celia asked.

Eileen rolled her eyes. "Since we got Annie, I've never had so many conversations about butch-femme. But you know, I say what I've always said. There's only one test and it's got nothing to do with babies. You're femme if you don't fart in front of your lover."

"Don't be gross," Chrissie said over Renee and Celia's laughter.

"No, no, I think she's onto something," Renee said with exaggerated eagerness. "I think there's a Sarah Lawrence master's thesis in it. Real Femmes Don't Fart: The Sociopolitical Construct."

"Careful – the lesbian seriousness police will get you yet, honey," Celia teased.

"Speaking of butch, though, you don't hear from Mike anymore, do you?" Renee asked.

Chrissie got up abruptly and punched the tape out of the VCR harder than seemed necessary. "No, not since we moved."

"I'm sorry . . . did I say the wrong thing?" Renee asked, looking to Celia for some direction, but she just shrugged.

"No, it's not your fault," Chrissie said, turning around. "I just. . . ." She shook her head. "I still hate him for what he did to Eileen and the house. She loved that house – and he wrecked it. And who was going to bring a baby to live there if he was going to keep hanging around? You know, it's one thing if you want to take chances for yourself. But I wouldn't have put it past him, I wouldn't have put much past him after what he did." She pursed her lips. "I wasn't going to test his limits with a baby on the scene. If I thought anything could ever happen to her –"

She covered her face and gave in to the fit of crying Renee had thought she seemed on the edge of all night. Eileen got up and wrapped her arms around her. Renee saw them — parents, a family — crossed over that threshold to a place she had never gone. And probably never would. She would never say this out loud — maybe not even to Celia — but she was angry at them for making her feel left behind.

Eileen walked them out to their car to review again the directions back to Brooklyn. Renee, behind the wheel because Celia had driven here, assured her for about the ninth time that they really had had a good time.

"Well, I have to be sure. I know everyone doesn't share my suburban wet dream," she said, rubbing the tops of her arms for warmth against the April night air.

They were all still waving as Renee pulled out of the driveway; ahead of them, the road disappeared into inky blackness. Why there were no streetlights outside the city proper was beyond her. That alone could keep her within city confines the rest of her life: insufficient night lighting everywhere else.

"So?" Celia said as they turned the corner.

Renee looked over at her. "So, what?"

"Do you want one?"

Renee smiled. "Do *you*?"

"I asked you first."

"You sound like a second-grader."

"Even so."

This was not the first time she and Celia had talked about children, but she knew they both felt they must continue to check in, to see if the other had begun to waver. "I think I'm destined to be a politically incorrect lesbian. I never wanted a cat and now I don't want a baby."

Celia took Renee's right hand off the wheel and held it in her lap. "I think if I could have one with you — I mean, if we could make one together, I'd want one. Is that terrible?"

Renee shook her head. "No, not terrible. Honest." She snapped on the radio. Celia's choice of music — an R&B station — was still tuned in. Renee changed it to country, the rule being that whoever was driving got to choose the station. Renee grinned and Celia winced as the twangy ballad filled the car. Celia, Renee knew, could tolerate the country station far less than she herself could the R&B. "I swear, I think we're secretly an interracial couple."

"You're changing the subject," Celia said.

"You think lack of musical compatibility is not a serious consideration if we were going to have a kid together?" Silhouettes of large houses with windows lit like watching eyes slid past the car. She felt bone-deep content: Celia beside her in the cozy dark of the car, another weekend morning of sleeping late still ahead of her.

"Little straight girls start fantasizing about being a mother when they're about four," Celia said. "They make lists of names. They line up doll clothes. They debate how many years apart their kids should be. I never did that, ever. I have absolutely no memories of a single moment like that. Is that because I knew from early on that I wasn't going to have the kind of life where I could make children with my husband? Did I rule it out because it wasn't possible, so I never let myself even want it?"

We did this, Renee thought, a brief but sharp pinpoint of anger piercing the happy bubble of her mood. We examined every stirring, every feeling we ever had under the microscope of our sexuality. Did we like the color green because we were gay? Was it being a lesbian that made us choose a certain perfume? "I don't know," Renee said, flipping open the vent. "But what's the point of supposing? You're *not* straight."

"The point is, do you think there's something wrong with us because we don't want kids?"

"Do we have to want them just because it's now possible to adopt them?" Renee said.

"You're not answering the question."

Renee watched the highway traffic, with its pattern of crisp red tail lights and, to her left, the streaky white headlights of on-coming cars. She wasn't in the mood for this conversation. She didn't even know what this conversation was *about.* "Are you trying to tell me you want kids?" she asked, not disguising her irritation.

"And what if I were?"

Renee felt her stomach crimp in fear. She took her eyes off the road and looked over. "Celia," she hissed. "Don't joke."

"Look, I don't really think I want kids," Celia said, looking out her window. She sounded weary. "But I'd like to think we'd do it if I wanted it. Sometimes I just feel . . ."

"Feel what? Just feel *what?*" Renee demanded.

"That we don't do something unless *you* want to."

"Like *what?*"

"Like ever move out of Brooklyn or start a

127

business together or even go to a movie you don't want to see."

Renee studied the moving grid of crimson tail lights in front of her; she was afraid, suddenly, of hidden hazards all around. "Movies aside, honey, if any of these are things you want to do, you know we can talk about them. I really don't know where this is all coming from." She heard the note of pleading in her own voice and was embarrassed. She felt prepared to beg, but she didn't know for what exactly.

"I don't know where it's coming from, either," Celia said, turning back to her with a sudden smile. "I'm just moody tonight. Forget it."

Renee knew it was probably reckless to take her at her word, but she did, and was relieved to focus fully on the tangible dangers of traffic.

On Monday morning, Renee stood on the subway platform, waiting for the F train into Manhattan. She watched a couple further down the platform who were arguing. The woman looked past the man as she spoke, letting him know that time, the train, her destination, were all more important than he was. He leaned in and talked down at the top of her head, letting her know that his height, his bulk, his strength were all superior to hers. His mouth moved in tight-lipped anger; his eyes were squinted, as if at a target.

Renee kept watching: they withdrew. She imagined the woman thinking: *Never mind about it, he didn't finish his coffee this morning, is all.* She thought mildly about the day ahead . . . and how she'd make him a nice dinner tonight. He leaned back into his newspaper, folded into a square shield, and Renee imagined him thinking: *My God, of all the women I could have had. . . . That's it, starting today I'm leaving, in increments, until she doesn't care any more, than I'll go for real, for good.*

The train screeched into the station; they linked hands and stepped on. To anyone else, they looked just fine. But Renee knew. Renee knew better.

Renee was on dishwashing duty because Celia had cooked, and the rule was, whoever didn't cook, cleaned. Renee hated dishwashing slightly less than ironing, but only because she despised ironing with an almost physical revulsion. And yet she was a slave to stiffly pressed clothes and shiny pots. She understood that she was in conflict with her own desires.

It wasn't so bad doing the dishes when Celia stayed in the kitchen, even if the two of them said nothing to each other. It was as if there was between them a common energy field; when they were apart, she noticed a perceptible drain, a kind of jangling of the nerves. But as usual, they had gotten in from work late, finished dinner late, and there was a TV movie on that Celia wanted to see, so she'd gone in to the bedroom ahead of her.

The hot water and the scrub pad would have her nail polish chipped by the time she was done, Renee knew, which meant twenty minutes blown taking it all off and putting fresh coats on. The maintenance of a professional look was ongoing and exhausting, in scores of small daily ways — the handwashing of stockings, the pressing of skirts, the application of mascara. Sometimes she fantasized about working someplace ten minutes from the house, someplace where she could wear jeans every day and not feel the pinch of pumps or the sweaty bondage of stockings. Sometimes these work-freedom fantasies, as she came to think of them, were more intense and sensual than her sex fantasies, although they were also more melancholy because they seemed even less likely to ever be realized.

She shut off the kitchen faucet; silencing the running water gave her a small thrill. She padded slowly down the hall and stood in the threshold watching Celia in bed, already undressed, leaning against a chaos of unmatched throw pillows, her face set in the passive pleasure of TV hypnosis.

"Any good?" Renee said, feeling herself drawn to the bed despite her good intentions of going to her desk and reading over some papers she'd dragged home from the office.

"It just started," Celia said, absentmindedly patting the bed next to her, summoning, a siren song of idle release.

Renee laid herself across the bed gratefully, put her head on Celia's stomach. She always took grave comfort in this, her cheek against the slight swell, feeling her head go faintly up and down with Celia's breathing, and grazing a fingertip along the fine blonde hairs of her belly. "Are we okay?" she asked.

"Hmmm? Are we what?" Celia asked.

"Are we okay."

"Of course, babe. What's the matter? Come up here where I can see you."

"I keep thinking about Saturday night," Renee said, sitting up to face her.

"Don't. It was nothing, I told you."

"We can have a baby if you want."

Celia smiled, wrapped Renee's long hair loosely around her wrist. "I didn't really mean all that. I know it's not true that we always do things your way. I just . . . I needed to blame someone." She pursed her lips in a way Renee knew was self-reproaching. "I'm sorry."

"So we're okay?"

"Yes, silly." Renee submitted to Celia's hands, which were piling her hair up on top of her head exposing the back of her neck, raking goosebumps into her skin.

"Blame someone for what, though?" Renee asked.

"I'm not sure," Celia said.

Renee put her head in Celia's lap again and studied Celia's jawline, her blonde hair, trying to calculate in her mind's eye — the way computers can age the photo of a missing child — what a baby who resembled both of them might look like. What must that feel like: the chance to submit to that great mystery, part romance, part biology, of a child born of their loins, of life springing from their commingled lives? Why had nature conspired against them, not given them this miracle?

"Do you wonder what she'd look like, though?" Renee whispered.

"No. How can you imagine something that's not possible?" She looked back at the television.

Renee rolled over, put her cheek back against Celia's belly, felt sleep unraveling her thoughts slowly into the languid chaos of dreams, and felt baby kisses, the color of tulips, the scent of lavender, raining weightlessly onto her head, down into daydreams, down into memory.

SAFE SEX

"Don't we know each other?" Tess says to the waitress after giving her order.

"Yes, about a year ago, we went out once ..." The waitress, shapely in a black mini-skirt and black Spandex top, trails off hesitantly. Her earlobes turn pink and she glances at Celia and me nervously, checking, I suspect, for signs of ridicule or silent warning.

"Oh, well, then we should do it *again*," Tess says with the ferocious enthusiasm she brings to most conversations, even those with perfect, or near-perfect, strangers. "Before we leave, give me your number." She drops a slim-fingered hand intimately onto the woman's forearm. "Or better yet, you'll tell me if you have any plans after you get off work tonight."

The waitress grins broadly and nods, as if her life has not had meaning until this moment, and scurries away with our order.

Tess sits up straighter in her chair, angles a little closer to us on her elbows. "I can't remember if I did her or not, but I have a feeling it'll all come back to me later."

Celia and I laugh and mildly scold, as is expected of us as the reigning long-term, monogamous couple in our circle. But before I met Celia, Tess and I were cruising buddies. Freshly sprung from college, I set upon the Manhattan lesbian bar scene with the hunger of a fallen Slim-Fast devotee set loose in Balducci's. Not that I didn't have my share of affairs in college but they played like *Little House on the Prairie* compared to the ruthless cruising and chaotic couplings and uncouplings that went on in the city among twentysomething lesbians in the early eighties. I made the mistake for about two weeks of thinking I might have been in love with Tess until I realized there was a revolving door on her heart. I got the picture quickly enough so that there was not much damage done, and after that I was happy to hang onto her coattails at clubs, since there were always more than enough women collected around Tess than even Tess could handle in one night. Our relationship remained an odd sort: we were not quite ex-lovers (can you be an ex-lover if you slept with a woman only twice?) and not quite friends. Our conversations more closely resembled Wall Street stock trading (we regularly tracked the rising or falling fortunes of the women we dated, wanted to date, would never date, or wouldn't date us) than anything having to do with soul-baring. And yet, we were a little bit of both, and that was the toehold of a genuine affection that grew.

"So how are the two of you — *really?*" Tess asks us, touching the backs of our hands, insistent and concerned. Unlike our other single friends, Tess neither pines after our hallowed state of togetherness nor derides it as bourgeois bunk. She maintains instead a respectful but long-distance admiration, as if we have evolved to a higher state along the reincarnation chain than she should be expected to match in her own lifetime.

Celia and I mumble a few highlights of our domestic bliss, including the jewelry we got each other for our anniversary last weekend, but we are all impatient, since what we have really gathered together for in this, our roughly bi-monthly dinner with Tess, is to be an audience for her tales of lesbian lasciviousness in the Big City.

The waitress, her red-blonde hair obviously freshly combed, comes back with our drinks and, I notice, struggles to keep her face set, to maintain whatever thin membrane remains of anonymous-service-worker-to-paying-customer, when it's clear that she wishes she were sitting in Tess's lap instead. "Thanks, darling," Tess says breathily when the waitress puts the martini down in front of her. "Remind me of your name."

"Tammy," the waitress says quietly, making eye contact only with Celia and me before running off again. I notice she does not need to be reminded of Tess's name.

"You've got her rattled," I say.

"I know, and I love it," Tess says, leaning back in her wooden chair.

Tess is not what you would call traditionally pretty; her nose is a little too long, her eyes a little too wide-set, but you wouldn't notice this at all unless you were coolly — maybe even coldly — appraising her, because Tess, The Presence, is so much more than the sum of her parts. She has the kind of charm that wins elections, a way of looking at women that lets them know that the sex will be dazzling, and gives them hope that love won't be far behind. (In fact, my memory of her in bed is a bit hazy, but I know that there were candles and feathers and white mousse, not necessarily in that order, not necessarily in their preordained roles.) Her long hair is blonde and though I have never bothered to ask if it's natural, Celia is the one who assures me that of course it isn't. Tess is partial to sheer or very unbuttoned blouses, tight, cigarette-legged jeans, which she can get away with even now, since she seems to have lost a pound for every one I have gained in the sure and silent march toward middle-age.

First there is the requisite review of the women she was dating when last we met, to see who has survived the test of months. Not Alix. "She was so lazy that if she could have hired someone to have fun for her she would have," says Tess. Not Suzanne. "She was only horny when she was pre-menstrual and

136

I just couldn't drop everything to work her into my schedule all the time." Not even Gwen, which disappoints me the most, because Tess had come close to saying genuinely emotional things about her. "Suffocated me," Tess now says dismissively, delicately fingering her white throat. Despite her serial declarations that "this might be the one" (and I still nearly believe along with her each time) her passions come and go like summer rainstorms, unpredictable and inconsequential.

For a long while after I got serious about Celia, I continued to wish the same good fortune for Tess, to counsel her with an eye toward long-term commitment, to even fix her up with other friends of mine who were looking to some day soon shop for a sofa bed with the woman of their dreams. It was Celia who forced me to consider that Tess had no intention of ever being anything but perpetually single.

Of course, single does not mean alone, which Tess never is. Tess is the only woman I know who, when she says she is double-dating, means that both women are with her. In fact, that is literally what she is entangled in now, she tells us. She is the "other woman" to two women, and the two women live together. Of course, neither knows the other is cheating, let alone with the other's mistress. Only Tess knows both their secrets, and I can see that the perversity of the situation is as much of a turn-on for her as the individual women themselves. Maybe more.

"Tess, is there never to be a walk to the altar in all white for you?" I ask.

She pushes her hair back over her shoulder to try the soup a sub-waiter has brought over. "First of all, white is not my color, you know that. But seriously, I've been having a *great* time. And what I really want, what I still haven't found, is a woman who, when she walks into the room, makes my heart pound and sweat break out on my temples."

"Maybe you've confused love with an anxiety attack," I say.

Celia sputters on her soup at this observation, but tries to pretend it's just too hot. She fans at the soup bowl elaborately. "What about safe sex?" she asks.

"Celia, honey, for me, safe sex means not getting caught by her angry butch lover." Tess laughs huskily.

"No, come on." Celia has not ever come right out and admitted that she disapproves of Tess's carnivorous lifestyle — she wouldn't like to see herself as prudish in any way — but I can tell that's how she feels.

"Look, if all it came down to was sucking on plastic wrap, I'd rather stay home and watch videos, you know?" She laughs again, prompting the two gay men at the next table to raise their wine glasses her way in a toast. Tess raises her martini glass in kind. "The boys," she says, putting her hand over her cleavage. "My heart breaks for them. I don't think I could ever be that disciplined."

"Maybe you could if it was a matter of life and death." Celia has lost most of her sense of humor by now; I tap her ankle under the table as a warning.

"No, life without sex *is* death," Tess says. She puts her martini glass to her lips without taking her eyes off either of us.

* * * * *

After we order dessert, Tess excuses herself. I watch her follow Tammy over to the bar, where she is standing with her order pad, reading off it to the bartender. Tess puts her hand on Tammy's small waist and then they dissolve into the shadows at the back of the restaurant. Watching her, I'm suddenly bereft that I can't follow, that I, too, can't pluck some moist-lipped waitress in a short skirt away from the bar and run my hand up the foreign, black-stockinged inside of her taut thigh.

The sub-waiter comes over again, bringing me and Celia the pecan pie we are sharing, and leaves Tess's Mexican coffee.

"Envy her? Even a little bit?" Celia says, lopping off the tip of the pie eagerly.

"No, of course not, on the contrary," I say with complete conviction.

"It's okay, you can tell me. Just a little bit?"

"*No,*" I say, testily. "For me, the search had a purpose. For Tess, the search *is* the purpose."

"Tammy's kind of cute, though, isn't she? In a strawberry-blonde kind of way."

"Flavor of the week, in Tess's case."

"I guess that's what's wrong with safe sex," Celia says. "Everyone knows that dangerous sex is sexy. Not safety."

My breath catches a little, since I wonder if Celia is talking about us, but I can't ask, because Tess is back at the table now, her lips shiny red with fresh lipstick, her hair smooth and orderly. "Well, I have my after-dinner drink all booked. Seems Tammy's place is only a few blocks from here. Of course, I had to do a little test run first to see if it was a good idea."

139

"What do you mean?" I ask.

"I took her into the bathroom and said I wanted to see if I recognized her from her kiss. Of course, I don't remember her from Mata Hari, but it was a *very* nice kiss."

We laugh appreciatively. Celia seems to be in a better mood suddenly and I don't know whether to credit it to the pecan-pie sugar rush or if she's just regained her manners. Tess's confession reminds me of the night I arranged a dinner with several of my single friends, Tess included, though I wasn't playing matchmaker; I was merely trying to take care of a string of social obligations with one meal, since I was, by that time, involved with Celia and my free time had to be more carefully budgeted. Without my catching on until much later — or anyone else at the table catching on, for that matter — Tess had somehow gotten each of the women in turn to follow her into the bathroom, for a long kiss and God knows what else, so she could decide which of them she wanted to ask for a phone number.

When I remind Tess of this stunt, she is delighted with herself all over again. "It's true, I do some of my best work in bathrooms." She samples her Mexican coffee, looking pensive. "Hey, Tammy doesn't get off work for another two hours," Tess says. "Want to head over to the Clit Club for a while?"

I look at Celia, who looks at her watch, and who is the designated driver back home to Brooklyn. "I don't know," she says. "It's eleven-thirty. I've got a racquetball game at eight in the morning."

This is a bald-faced lie, I know, so I get the message loud and clear that Celia, for whatever reason, is ready to go home. "Sorry," I say to Tess. "That's life in the boroughs. But I somehow don't think you'll be lonely too long at the Club."

"Well, if you guys don't go, I might just hang here at the bar," she says, looking over her shoulder, "and keep an eye on Tammy."

"Oh, really?" I say, raising an eyebrow skeptically.

"I'm allowed to feel possessive the first forty-eight hours," Tess says, winking.

We are in the left lane of the Brooklyn-Queens Expressway when all the tension goes out of the car. We start to coast as though we are slowing for a light and the headlights of the car behind us swallow up the rearview mirror as it speeds closer to our rear end.

"What are you *doing*? Why are you slowing down?" I say, leaning forward in my seat, as if that could somehow propel us forward.

Celia is glaring at the dashboard. "We're out of gas."

"Out of *gas*? How could be we be out of *gas*? Jesus, ease over," I say, swiveling around to look behind us into the middle lane, feeling panic start to warm its way up my neck.

Celia has clicked on the hazards and manages to calmly steer while horns blare. We leisurely waft across the lanes to the extreme right and whatever narrow shoulder there is. The car stops practically without Celia's foot touching the brake. Traffic quickly snarls up behind us.

We sit in pissed-off silence for a few minutes,

trying not to feel ridiculous. Then I start. "How could you not have noticed we were so low on gas when you got in the car?"

"*Me?* How could you not have noticed when you got *out* of the car that you'd used nearly every last goddamn drop — and tell me that I might want to fill up before we left Manhattan!"

"I'm not in charge of the ride home — *you* are. Don't try to palm this off on me."

"Unbelievable."

"You've been driving for fifteen minutes! Didn't you notice? Don't you ever check your speed? Your eyes might have — just possibly — grazed over the gas meter once or twice, for God's sake."

"Un-fucking-believable." Celia falls back hard against the seat.

"Well, come on, let's go," I boom. "We can't sit here all night. We'll just have to walk to the nearest phone."

"Bullshit, we will. You don't just *stroll* along the BQE. Not unless you want to know what it feels like to be a human bull's eye."

We both sit, frowning hard, as cars to our left hurtle by on their uninterrupted journeys toward warm beds and waiting houses. The knick-knock of the hazards signal seems to grow louder in my ears.

"You have another idea, then?" I say. "I'm waiting to hear it."

"That's just it," Celia says. "We wait."

"Wait? *Wait.* So you've become religious. You believe in miracles now? The car is going to fill up with gas by itself. And loaves and fishes will appear in the back seat."

She looks at me in a truly unfriendly way that

scares me. Sometimes I wonder to myself — because I would never say it aloud out of superstition that that would give it power, like a spark exposed to air — if the best between us is past. It's a remote terror, easily dismissed, something I chalk up to a hundred little annoyances and disappointments, plenty of which have nothing even to do with Celia, but just make my picture of the world that much less ideal. And then I wonder, What thoughts does Celia have that she keeps silent, buried, from me? And do they matter, then, at all? Or do they have a shadow life? Do they seep like poison into the soil we are building our life on together?

"We should probably invest in a car phone," I say, making my voice more conciliatory.

We discuss prices and logistics for a while, both of us glancing regularly into the rear- and side-view mirrors for an angel of mercy in any form. I lean against the headrest and let myself relax. "Tess and Tammy kind of has a nice ring to it, don't you think?"

Celia rolls her eyes and we both laugh. "Can you believe she takes her into the bathroom for a test drive? It blows my mind."

I sidle closer, take her chin in my hand. "I wonder what she said to her? 'I knew from the moment I ordered the shrimp scampi that I wanted to make love to you.' " I kiss Celia though we are both laughing, feeling myself warm to the exercise. "You know, since we're stranded here, maybe we should take advantage of the back seat. Weren't you saying something at dinner about the appeal of dangerous sex?" I lean in to kiss her again when suddenly there is insistent knocking on Celia's

143

window and a painful white light explodes in my eyes.

We yank away from each other, and Celia slides the window down. There stands a hulking cop with a flashlight.

"What seems to be the problem here?" The voice reveals the cop to be a woman, something that, given the bulky blue jacket, the hat, and the blunt features, I wouldn't have been able to guess. This is exceptional enough that the moment takes on a freeze-frame stillness.

"We've, uh, run out of gas," Celia says, meekly, I know, because she realizes the cop had to have seen us kissing.

The cop considers this, then smiles broadly and winks. "It didn't look that way to me." We are both too stunned to laugh — something we regret later — and instead just stare stupidly. "Hang on. I've got a can of gas. I can give you enough to get to the nearest station at the next exit."

While the cop busies herself at the back of our car, Celia and I sit like chastened school children, stunned at our luck on both counts. "You know," I say, "we should reward the fates. We should get her phone number for Tess."

Celia looks disoriented for a second, then breaks into animated laughter. We manage to get control of ourselves by the time the cop is looming in the window again.

"What do we owe you for that?" Celia asks.

"Nothing. Just get yourself to a gas station," she says. "Then home." She winks again.

"Yes, ma'am," Celia says.

The cop pats the roof affectionately and stomps back to her own car.

This time it takes us much longer to stop laughing. By the time we get to the station, my sides ache.

On our answering machine, when we get home, is a message from Tess. We can hear the boisterousness of the restaurant in the background. "Hi, guys. Great seeing you both, as always." Here she stops to inhale hard on her cigarette; we can hear the sharp intake, as if she is startled by something. "I've been sitting here watching Tammy. She's *very* cute." I imagine Tess's eyes following Tammy as she travels back and forth from table to bar, all mystery and undiscovered secrets. How unjudgmental we are in those first few unselfish moments, when the desired is perfect even in all her flaws, because that is simply the way she is.

"I was thinking, maybe I should settle down, too," Tess says on the tape, nearly convincing me again. Then she laughs her contagious, delighted laugh. "She really could be the one, you know. What do you two think?"

NOT TELLING MOTHER

Almost as soon as I get there, my mother takes out the box. She makes us sit at the kitchen table, the box between us like some unearthed treasure, full of someone else's neglected fortunes she has guiltily come by.

"This one is me and my brother when we were kids," she says, offering a small, rectangular photograph. The photo is black-and-white, as all the photos in the battered shirt box seem to be, all of them crowded and tumbled in like a spilled deck of cards, rising into a slight mound at the center.

146

In this picture, my uncle is about ten or twelve, already sleekly handsome, with the same tight-lipped smile he still has today, in his sixties. My mother is dark, nearly swarthy, her hair pulled into thick, unruly pigtails. She is smiling hard, and I wonder who was behind the camera. I ask, but she doesn't recall.

"This is my mother," she says, holding out another one, "with her six sisters." I pick out my grandmother right away. She is plumper, darker-haired and more rested than she looked by the time I was old enough to notice these things. She is standing, unsmiling, partly obscured by one of her younger sisters, a blonde with a big grin and conspicuous earrings. My grandmother, I realize after scanning the other sisters' faces, actually looks grim. This may be because she never enjoyed having her picture taken, or it may be that the photo was taken after her husband had left her, or after a particularly exhausting week at the laundry where she worked. But my mother and I have no real idea; we just guess.

"You know, Grandma was never one to cry on a shoulder. She had that ulcerated leg after she moved in with us and she never let me take her to the doctor. I used to hear her in her room at night, moaning. But she'd deny it in the morning, like I'd accused her of a crime. I think she just got used to living with a certain level of pain. Not that you don't notice – that's crap – but you don't expect things to get any better."

My mother quickly fishes out another one – she's obviously got her favorites set aside to show me first – and puts it on the table in front of me.

"My mother at about twenty, I guess," she says. "Can you believe I never saw a picture of her that young before now? She never kept pictures around." We both stare, a little reverently, at the shot. She is a full-blown flapper here, a silent film star with her bowl-cut hairstyle and a hat cocked over one eye. Her lips look pouty with some dark lipstick and her eyes are heavy-lidded and sly. This would be before she was married, when all things, perhaps, still seemed possible. I turn the picture over, hunting for clues: 1926 is written in a corner in ink that has turned brown. The depression would not come for another three years, my mother not for another eight.

"Amazing," I say, meaning that this is the first time my mother has seen a photo like this. Myself, I'm a cataloguer. On vacations, I take well-framed photos and keep a travel diary I use for informative album captions later. The thought of not seeing pictures of my parents in their youth would have been intolerable. The photos are a kind of proof. Like tribal people who forbid their picture being taken, I, too, believe a photo can steal the soul, but unlike them, I'm grateful.

"How'd it go?" Celia asks me as soon as I'm inside the front door. She is curled on the couch with her checkbook and bills in her lap.

"Fine. We looked at the old pictures."

"That means you didn't tell her."

I go over to the couch where she's sitting and run my hand through her blonde curls, from the nape of her neck forward. "There are a lot of things I don't tell her."

"Renee, we've been over this. We agreed this was the perfect night, with your dad out bowling."

I sit down next to her, extraordinarily grateful for this simple pleasure: I didn't realize how tired I was. It's true that we had agreed on this; telling both my parents at one time seemed more of an effort than I could handle. "What can I tell you? There never seems to be a good segue into, Hey, Mom, by the way, I'm a dyke."

"Don't joke."

"I'm not. I'm serious. Besides, she probably already knows."

"That's not the same as telling her."

I lean back and put my feet up on the glass coffee table. The table is ours, we own it together, just like we own everything in the apartment together. We have one bed in a two-bedroom place. My mother knows all this and still we say nothing. She loves Celia and that's the part that scares me the most.

Celia fantasizes rewards for telling but I see none. In the highly acute way of children who have never been allowed to grow up in their parents' imagination, I know how total and furious a disappointment the news would be. Whatever small and selfish reward that might be salvaged after years of pain would surely pale by comparison. I have come to believe it's better not to suffocate whatever short breaths of hope my mother is still able to draw.

"What if something happens to one of us? You know the stories. You want her to find out in an emergency room that I have power of attorney?"

Celia knows this argument makes my stomach flex like an accordion. The power of attorney was my idea. I have a lively imagination for sudden disaster — cars jumping curbs, pieces of well-aimed scaffolding plummeting to the sidewalk below.

"I'm working on it," I say. "This really isn't a great time, anyway, with Aunt Marcie just dying. She was the last of my grandmother's sisters, you know."

Celia gives me a dark look, the way you'd look at a stubborn child who's old enough to know better. "Aunt Marcie hasn't got a thing to do with this."

"Well, that's how she got the new box of photos and she's all excited about them. I didn't have the heart to spoil her fun. She's going to buy antique frames and put some of them up in the den." I get up, planning to head for the bathroom and bed. Celia catches my hand.

"Tell her, will you? Do it for me."

This is a low blow, of course, but Celia has no regrets. She rarely does.

"Aunt Marcie came in the mail today," my mother says very soon into our phone conversation. "By UPS, actually. I had to sign for it so I saw the address before I opened it and I thought, here I am, carrying Aunt Marcie across the room."

Aunt Marcie had asked to be cremated and my mother, as her closest living relative, got the ashes.

"It's heavier than I thought it would be and you can hear things rattling around in there. Bone fragments, I think."

"What's the container look like?"

"Like something you'd put file cards in and keep in an office. Except that it's sealed all around. And I had to sign something explaining the incineration process so I'd understand that I might have leftover ashes from someone else in with Aunt Marcie."

"Good God," I say. "Why would they think to tell you something like that? Who would have ever thought to ask about something like that?"

"I don't know. Maybe some people have rituals."

I shudder slightly and don't ask what she means.

"I don't know how I feel about cremation," my mother continues. "It's the same as donating your organs. How does anyone know we're not going to need these things after we're dead? Can you imagine being blind for eternity? I know it sounds silly, but no one knows for *sure*."

I admit it's true that no one knows for sure but I say that I feel reasonably certain we won't, and even if we did, there would probably be some kind of cosmic lost and found where you could get them back. Probably better ones, for being a good sport. My license, therefore, indicates that my organs can be donated.

"You know, some of the Hasidic Jews, when that rabbi was shot in Williamsburg, they picked up the whole slab of sidewalk with him to be buried. The whole thing was sacred, where it happened."

An image flashes across my mind of the crumpled body in wilted black robes atop its concrete bed, being carried by four men at each corner, the way the Pharaohs used to parade their kings through the village. "That seems extreme," I say.

"Well, it doesn't matter, anyway, what you check off on your license because the doctors ask the next of kin what they want to do since they're the ones who can sue and make trouble. I could overrule you," she says.

A mother's ultimate last word, I think. It's unsettling how much she knows these days about the official business of dying. But what she doesn't know is that Celia agrees with me about organ donation and she's my legal next of kin now.

But my mother has already changed the subject. "I got those picture frames. They call them oxidized. They're greenish and look really old but they're not old at all. Have you ever seen them?"

I tell her no, but that I can imagine exactly what they look like.

I never knew my mother's father. Actually, neither did she, not really. "He was just some stranger who came to see my mother every once in a while," she's fond of saying. My grandmother would make my mother kiss him when he came over and my mother hated that. Because when he came, he took my grandmother out with him, and one of the sisters, often Aunt Marcie, would babysit. My mother would only pretend to be asleep until my grandmother came home again. Unlike everything I've ever heard or read about absent or divorced or dead or deserting fathers, there was no hole blown open in my mother's family, or my mother's particular psyche. Instead, the sisters closed over the space where he used to be like a wave over a footprint; in a little while there was no trace of him at all.

This is the way my mother tells it, anyway. What my grandmother felt, we can only guess at. I used to try to get her to tell me things, when I still lived at home and we'd be having lunch together, alone. Did you miss him, I'd ask. If I was patient enough, she'd tell a hurried story. I remember one about the time she and my grandfather were first married and lived with his mother, and the old woman came upstairs in the middle of the night and threw their bedroom door wide open. Then just went back down the stairs. My grandmother eventually moved out; my grandfather stayed. But she usually says he left her. I guess it's the same thing: If you're not with me, you're against me.

So it's odd to come across these photos of him in the box when I go to my mother's again. My parents are away in Atlantic City overnight and I'm in charge of the dog. She's an overweight Labrador who likes to press her hindquarters against my legs so I'll scratch her back. When I first moved out, she held a grudge. More than my mother, I think. She'd sit at the far end of the living room when I'd come over, glowering, reproaching. I took it hard. Now we've both adjusted.

In the photos, my grandfather is dark, stocky, a man's man, not completely trustworthy-looking —

though it's possible I'm making this last part up, ascribing the stories to the face.

I pull the photos out in clumps, sifting through them on the seat of the couch next to me as if I expect them to fit together in some order, to tell a coherent story, spell out some truth. I recognize the players, some of whom my mother has described. The cousin who became a nun and died of a brain hemorrhage at twenty-six. The alcoholic uncle who was convicted of manslaughter after hitting someone drunk-driving. Aunt Marcie's husband who became a cop and shot open the door she had locked against one of his rages. Another uncle who raised pigeons, was rejected by the Army and never married.

It's possible that they are not such a motley crew, possible that these wounds and disgraces just made better stories and so are the ones that stuck. We are all many things, after all, but people, especially families, like some single, manageable theory to explain a person's whole life, all the choices, triumphs, miseries. I don't want to make my mother the one with the lesbian daughter.

What's hardest about telling — about not telling, actually — is that I have to make the choice for both of us, decide if our silence on the subject is mutual and comfortable, or if we are tied together at the ankle, perched at the edge of the same diving board, each terrified to give the other a shove. It's the fall we're afraid of as much as the impact, or maybe it's that the view from there is completely different and unknown, and the previous vantage point can never be regained.

The dog comes over and leans her rump against my knees. I scratch her back and she does an appreciative two-step with her hind legs, letting out a low grumbling moan. When my hand gets tired and I stop, she turns and looks at me like a little kid when the quarter on the rocking horse machine runs out.

In books and old movies, people take a loved one's ashes and sprinkle them over the Gulf of Mexico or the cliffs of Dover or someplace equally poetic. My mother does not go for such gestures. Instead, she has kept the file box in the garage and arranged for the cemetery to bury it for three hundred dollars next to Aunt Marcie's husband, the cop who shot the door open.

Celia has come with me and my mother, who looks pretty in her two-piece blue suit and her hair freshly colored and styled. The three of us stand near the headstone contemplating the steel box. It looks like some kind of perverse midget coffin out here on the grass under the sun. The gravedigger will come later, after we've gone, to dig the hole and deposit the box. For now, we improvise our own ceremony. My mother puts the bouquet of pink and white carnations, arranged in the shape of a cross, midway between the headstone and the box. Religious symbols still have power for her, even though she hasn't been to church in thirty years. Not that she hasn't wanted to, but as a young wife she made the mistake of confessing to a priest that she used birth control and was promptly disinvited. I've told her that they would probably let her come back now but the damage's been done, she's told me; the church wasn't there for her when she needed it.

"Let's say a prayer," she says, coming over to stand next to me. It's a warm June day, too sunny and blue-skyed for sorrow. She bows her head, shuts her eyes and takes my hand. I take Celia's hand on my other side and we all stand in silence. I hardly knew Aunt Marcie but a knot of grief lodges in my throat anyway.

"I like to think of the sisters all together again," my mother says after a while.

Celia presses my hand imperceptibly. I've told her that my mother has said how all the sisters, as they aged, never talked much about their husbands, often dead before them. Instead they talked and dreamt and worried about each other, drawn together by the same chemistry that makes twins lead parallel — even if separate — lives.

My mother's chin is quivering and I know she's struggling not to cry. So am I; like not telling, not crying is a family tradition. But I know what she's thinking; she's thinking about her own mother, my grandmother, and so am I. But what we are thinking is probably not the same. Because I am thinking: loving my grandmother was something we had in common, was probably the last time we loved a woman in something of the same way.

Celia has gone to sleep ahead of me, knocked out by the drive from Long Island after a day of polite conversation with my mother. Celia goes to sleep like a stone sinking to the bottom of a lake; I, on the other hand, struggle and writhe until I'm weary enough to lie still.

But tonight I can't sleep at all and I go downstairs to my photo albums. No crumpled shirt boxes for me; I have chronologically ordered leather-bound albums, each page dated and captioned. I pull down one of the recent ones with pictures from a vacation Celia and I took to California. I find the photo I want almost immediately: it shows me and Celia on the deck of a friend's house outside San Francisco. We are both tan and a little dewy-looking from the sun and wine and laughter. Her arm is around my shoulder, and I am holding the hand that dangles down and pressing it to my lips.

I carry the photo to the kitchen table and write a note. *Dear Mom, a picture of us. Love, Renee and Celia.* I put it in an envelope and address it. I go out the front door, determined to get to the mailbox before I lose my nerve.